I0677492

MOUNTAIN JACK PIKE

COMANCHE COME-ON

#3

Also by Robert J. Randisi

Angel Eyes

Tracker

Mountain Jack Pike

MOUNTAIN JACK PIKE

COMANCHE COME-ON

#3

Robert J. Randisi

SPEAKING VOLUMES, LLC

NAPLES, FLORIDA

2012

Comanche Come-On: #3

Copyright © 1989 by Robert J. Randisi

Originally published under the name Joseph Meek

All rights reserved. No part of this book may be reproduced or transmitted in any form or by any means without written permission of the author.

ISBN 978-1-61232-594-1

PROLOGUE

ONE

"Are you sure about this?" Jack Pike asked.

"Would I tell you I was if I wasn't?" Skins McConnell replied.

Pike gave his friend Skins a dubious look.

"If it meant money," Pike said, "you'd match me up with a grizzly bear."

"Naw . . . I wouldn't . . ." McConnell said, but then he fell silent and Pike wondered if he'd given his friend an idea.

"Give me your shirt," McConnell said.

Pike took off his shirt and handed it to McConnell.

In front of them some men were drawing a circle in the dirt.

"What's this guy you matched me up with look like?" Pike asked.

"I don't know."

"You don't know?"

McConnell shrugged.

"I just told them you'd take on their best man."

"That's great," Pike said. "What if their best man *is* a grizzly bear?"

5

"Come on, Jack," McConnell said, "stop talking about a grizzly bear."

Pike and McConnell were in a settlement in Colorado River Country and they were a little short of money. It was McConnell's idea that Pike wrestle somebody from the settlement, and then he would take bets on the match. Since Pike was six-four and weighed in at two hundred and forty pounds, they felt fairly safe in setting up the match.

Only now Pike was starting to get edgy. McConnell was much too close-mouthed and he had a feeling his friend knew something he didn't.

"How are we doing on bets?" Pike asked.

"Great," McConnell said. "Ain't a one bet on you."

"Nobody?" Pike said. That was odd. Surely his size alone would persuade some of the settlement dwellers to wager a dollar on him.

"Well . . . I had a drink with some boys and accidentally let on about your bad back."

"What bad back?"

"Exactly."

"You lied about my back?"

"Sure, I lied. I'm trying to get as much money bet against you as possible."

"That sounds like a lot of money, son," Pike said. "What if we lose?"

"Then we're gonna have to find a quick way out of this settlement, pronto."

The men had finished drawing the circle in the ground. The circle would actually be just a starting point. Once the match got going it would be rubbed out and the circle would then be formed by the spectators, and would widen as the need arose.

"You're looking good, Pike," McConnell said, patting his friend on the shoulder.

Pike looked at McConnell and said, "How come I get the feeling you're not as confident as you let on?"

"Don't worry about it," McConnell said. "It'll come out fine."

Pike was about to say something else when a man approached.

"Is your man ready?" the man asked McConnell.

"We're ready."

The man gave Pike the once-over and said, "Sure is a big man."

"Big enough," McConnell said.

At that the man laughed and walked away, shaking his head.

"What's he laughing at?" Pike asked.

"Nothing, nothing," McConnell said. "How you feeling?"

"Like I think you got me into something I don't want to get into."

"Relax," McConnell said, "relax."

Anything but relaxed, Pike looked over to the other side of the circle, trying to spot his opponent. He'd picked out two or three likely prospects when suddenly the crowd on the other side began to move aside, letting someone through.

Suddenly, Pike spotted a head and shoulders that towered above the other men, and then there he was, standing on the other side of the circle, looking right across at Pike.

"Jesus," Pike said in awe, "he is a grizzly bear."

McConnell too was staring at the man, even though he'd seen him once before. The first time he had seen him it was too late to call the match off, and now he was wondering if they shouldn't just turn tail and run.

The man they were staring at was easily six feet ten, and must have weighed about three-fifty or there-

7

abouts. He didn't have the muscle definition that Pike had; he was simply a mass of humanity, all on his own. He was raw-boned, thick in the middle, with sloping shoulders and beefy arms, and his legs looked like tree trunks.

"Skins—"

"I swear I didn't know, Pike," McConnell said. "Uh, not until it was too late, anyway."

"Too late is when I'm dead," Pike said, "and I ain't dead yet. Gimme my shirt."

He grabbed for the shirt, but McConnell pulled it away from his grasp.

"We can't pull out now," McConnell said. "You want to make these settlers think that mountain men are yella?"

"*This* mountain man is not yella," Pike said. "He's smart. I can't beat that monster, Skins."

"Sure you can, sure you can," McConnell said, putting his hands on Pike's shoulders and rubbing them. "You're quicker, and you've got to be smarter. He may look like a grizzly, but I bet he ain't as smart as one."

"Skins—"

"Pike, if you pull this off we'll have hundreds of dollars," McConnell said, "hundreds. We could take a vacation, maybe do some hunting. If we lose, we lose some money, that's all."

"That's all?" Pike asked. "*You* lose some money; I lose my head—and do you have the money to pay off all the bets?"

"Um, no."

"So you may lose your head, too."

"Pike, you can't pull out, for that very reason. We don't have the money."

"At least I'm alive now and we don't have the money," Pike said. "I can't bear the thought of him killing me and you having to face all these people

8

by yourself."

"Pike, I'm telling you," McConnell said, "you can beat him."

He looked across the circle and all the men there were laughing and patting the big man on the back, pointing across the way at Pike and McConnell.

"Whatsamatter, mountain man?" one of the settlers shouted. "Scared of Big Bubba?"

They all laughed aloud and pointed at them again. Pike began to burn slowly.

"See?" McConnell said. "They're making fun of you."

"Maybe," Pike said, thoughtfully, "if I can get him off his feet fast—"

"That's it, that's it," McConnell said. "Now you're talking."

"Step to the circle!" one of the settlers called. He had been chosen as a referee.

Pike stepped forward, into the circle.

"Don't forget the new rules, friend!" the same settler called out.

"New rules?" Pike asked. "What new rules, Skins?"

"Oh, I forgot to tell you," McConnell said. "I didn't want him getting his arms around you, so I had them change the rules."

"Change them to what?"

"Well, it's not really a wrestling match anymore, Pike."

"Then what is it, Skins?"

"Uh," McConnell began nervously, "no holds barred!"

"No holds barred?" Pike asked, his voice hoarse with disbelief.

McConnell slapped him on the back and said quickly, "Good luck."

9

TWO

"Fight!" the referee said.

In a no-holds-barred battle, that would be virtually all he would have to do.

The crowd around them immediately started a deafening din, rooting for their huge charge to finish Jack Pike quickly.

Pike moved to the center of the circle, still trying to figure what his strategy should be. The other man lumbered forward slowly, with a look of pure confidence. Pike was willing to bet that this man had never been whupped in his life—and had probably never even been off his feet.

Pike had faced some big men in his time—and beaten them—but he had never seen a man this big in his life.

Both men stopped and measured each other. Pike figured that the big man probably didn't respect him, and he was going to have to use that to his advantage. The lack of respect might make the big man careless.

He decided to lie back and make the big man come to him.

They circled each other a while longer until the crowd started to boo Pike for not rushing their man.

Pike could hear one voice above all of the others, and realized something The settler who had done all the talking before the fight was shouting instructions to the big man.

"Go and get him if he won't come to you!" the man shouted.

The big man nodded and moved toward Pike.

He lunged, his arms wide, and Pike had to duck low so that he wouldn't be inside those arms when they closed. He was inside, and took advantage of that fact by hitting the man three sledgehammer blows in succession, in the belly.

The big man grunted, but beyond that the blows didn't seem to have any effect. Pike moved back quickly, out of the man's reach. Body blows might have an effect after some time elapsed, but Pike was hoping to finish the fight before then—one way or another.

"Move in on him, but don't get careless!" the other man shouted. "Don't let him inside."

The big man nodded, and advanced on Pike a little more deliberately. Pike backed up but eventually he reached the circle of onlookers, and they didn't budge. He had no place to go but forward.

He sprang forward and threw a straight left into the man's face, hitting him on the nose. The man blinked, startled, and Pike followed with a hard right that landed flush on the man's jaw.

Big Bubba backed up a step.

"Don't back up!" the other man shouted. "He can't hurt you."

Big Bubba nodded, and moved forward. Pike tried another right, but the big man caught him by the arm and swung him around, letting go. Pike felt as if he had been shot out of a cannon. He careened toward the center of the circle, off balance and vulnerable,

11

but the big man did not move on him quickly enough to take advantage of the situation.

"Damn it, stay on him!" came the cry.

Big Bubba nodded and moved toward Pike, but in obeying one order he forgot the other, the one about not getting careless.

He swung wildly at Pike, who ducked beneath him and peppered him again with three hard blows to the belly. Bubba grunted, but stood his ground. He brought his fist down hard, trying to hit Pike in the back of the head, but Pike took the blow on his shoulder. As he danced away he felt as if his left arm had gone dead.

He circled the big man, shaking his arm, trying to work the feeling back into it.

"All right, all right!" the settler was shouting. "Respect him; he hits hard, but he cannot hurt you, Bubba!"

They went on like that for some time, Pike trying to get inside, land some punches, and then move away. Every so often Bubba would land a blow. Pike was starting to feel sore, and soon realized that one of Bubba's punches equaled about five of his own. At that rate he'd fall down from exhaustion before he could wear Bubba down—and all the while he could hear the other settler shouting instructions to the big man.

Pike was starting to think that part of the battle for Bubba was believing what the other man said—that he couldn't be hurt.

The other part of the battle was that the other man was doing all Bubba's thinking. If Bubba had had the other man's brain in his head, he would have been unbeatable.

Pike suddenly remembered how you kill a rattlesnake, and it applied here.

12

He circled a bit more until Bubba's back was to the man who was shouting instructions. He advanced then, throwing three lefts toward Bubba's face, but not hitting him.

"Back up, back up from those jabs!" the settler was yelling.

Bubba obeyed, which Pike was counting on. The big man backed up until he was almost on top of his friend. Pike backed off a bit, then lunged forward, telegraphing a right hand.

"Move, move to the side!" the settler shouted.

Bubba moved in plenty of time, but Pike threw the punch, anyway.

It landed flush on the settler's jaw. The man's head snapped back, his jaw snapped shut, and his eyes rolled up into his head.

Big Bubba turned and watched his "brain" slump to the ground. Stunned, he turned back to Pike just in time to catch a right on the jaw. Unprepared for the blow, his head snapped back and he started to fall into the crowd. Not wanting to be crushed, the crowd scattered, and instead of falling, Bubba began to back-pedal, fighting for his balance.

As he approached the lake, Pike decided to go for it. He ran forward and launched himself in a dive at the big man. He buried his shoulder in the man and heard the satisfied "whoosh" as the air emptied from the big man's lungs.

They went into the lake together, falling into the waist-deep water with Pike on top.

Pike recovered first and got to his knees—on the other man's chest. With Pike's weight on him, the big man couldn't get up, and was trapped under water. With the air gone from his lungs there wasn't much fight in him, and Pike stayed on top of him until he could feel the man growing limp. Not wanting to drown his opponent, he slid off him, reached beneath the surface, gathered a full head of hair and pulled the man's head above water. Just for show he hit the man once in the jaw, and then proceeded to pull him out of the water.

As dead weight, and in the water, Bubba was too much for Pike to handle alone.

"Give me a hand!" he called out, and several men moved into the water to help him.

"We got him, mister," one man said to him.

"Thanks."

"I ain't never seen anybody do that to Big Bubba," the man said, in awe. "Not nobody!"

Pike was too out of breath to reply.

He dragged himself out of the water and over to where Skins McConnell was happily collecting cash.

"You did it, boy, you did it," McConnell said. "I knew you could."

"Sure you did," Pike said, wiping water from his hair and beard.

McConnell continued to collect and someone handed Pike a towel, which he took with thanks. Finally, McConnell had collected on all his bets and he put the money away in his pocket.

"Let's get a drink and divvy up," McConnell said.

"Sounds good to me," Pike said. He wanted to drink enough to make him numb, so he wouldn't feel how sore he was. The morning was going to be a bitch.

"Tell me something," McConnell said, as they walked to the tent that was being used as a saloon until a saloon could be erected.

"What?"

"I mean, don't get me wrong," Skins said. "I knew you could do it—but how did you do it?"

"The guy who was doing all the shouting?"

"Yeah, the guy you knocked out by accident."

14

"That was no accident."

"No accident? What the hell did you hit him for?"

"You know how to kill a rattlesnake, don't you?"

"Of course I know how to kill a rattlesnake," McConnell said. "What's that got to do with anything?"

"Same principle," Pike said. "Cut off the head, and the body dies."

PART ONE

SETTLEMENT

CHAPTER ONE

"You look like hell," Kit Carson said to Jack Pike.
Pike laughed.

"You should have seen me three days ago," Pike said. After three days there was still some soreness from his fight with Big Bubba, but he felt better today—well enough to move on.

Carson had ridden in that afternoon, and Pike had immediately invited his old friend for a drink. In his party Carson had one other white man and three Delaware Indians.

"Where you heading with the Delaware?" Pike asked over the drinks.

"We're going down south to New Mexico, below the Arkansas River."

"Comanche country," Pike said. "What's there?"

"Good hunting, that's what."

The Delaware Indians, *en masse*, had patterned themselves after the white man, taking up his weaponry and his way of life. They differed from the whites only in their blood and their speech. Any time a white man needed a guide, he would usually turn to a Delaware. They combined the best parts of both men, red and white.

Of course, this made them the mortal enemy of the Plains Indians, who hated whites and so, by association, hated the Delaware.

More than anyone else—including other whites, the Mexicans, Spaniards, French Canadians and even the settlers—the mountain men accepted the Delaware on equal terms.

"You're asking for trouble from the Comanche," Pike said, "especially taking the Delaware along."

"It will add spice to the hunt," Carson said. "Why don't you come along?"

"I'm traveling with Skins McConnell."

"I know Skins," Carson said. "Bring him along."

"I'll put it to him," Pike said. "We were looking for a vacation, anyway."

"Good," Carson said. "Now tell me what happened three days ago."

Pike had just finished relating the facts of the fight when two men entered the tent. Carson saw them, one a huge man, and the other a man whose jaw was oddly swollen.

The two men advanced toward him and Pike, and Carson tensed.

"Is that him?"

"That's him," Pike said.

"You bested him?"

"You don't have to sound so surprised."

"Come on, my friend," Carson said, "there are few times I would ever bet against you, but if I had been here three days ago—"

"You would have lost money," Pike said, and then he added, "I got lucky."

"You might have to get lucky again," Carson said. "He looks like he's ready for a rematch."

"Nah," Pike said, "he always looks that way."

The two men reached him, and Pike saw that it was

20

the smaller man who was giving him the hard looks. He had not meant to hit the man that hard, but in the heat of battle he hadn't pulled his punch. As a result the other man had not been able to speak since then, and probably would not for a while.

However, Big Bubba, following the fight, had become very friendly toward Pike, almost like a huge child.

"Pike," Bubba said, dropping a hand the size of a bear paw on Pike's shoulder, "I buy you a drink."

Bubba's own speech had improved over the past three days, since the other man—whose name was Comfort—could no longer speak for him.

"Sure, Bubba," Pike said.

"This your friend?"

"Yes," Pike said. "Kit Carson."

"I buy him a drink, too."

Bubba looked at Carson, who readily agreed.

"I send them over," Bubba said and then he and Comfort walked to the bar.

"Looks like you made a friend," Carson said.

Pike looked over toward the bar, where Comfort was glaring at him. Not only had he damaged Comfort's jaw and embarrassed him, but the man had lost a lot of money.

"And an enemy, too, I'm afraid," he said.

Pike and Carson finished their drinks, then had the ones that Bubba sent over. While they were drinking those, Carson's friend came in with the three Delaware.

"That's Joe Stack," Carson said. "The Delaware are Mantooth, Jonesy and Tom Broad."

Stack and the three Delaware went to the bar and leaned their rifles against it. When Stack asked for a drink he was served. When he asked for drinks for the Delaware, the trouble started.

"I ain't serving no Indians," the settler bartender said.

Mountain men accepted the Delaware as equals, but to the settlers they were just Indians.

"Give them a drink," Pike heard Joe Stack say.

"I said I ain't servin' no Indians."

"I'm payin'," Joe Stack said.

"You can drink," the bartender said. "They can't."

Pike and Carson watched with interest.

"Give me another drink," Stack said.

"Sure," the bartender said, and poured Stack another drink.

Stack picked it up and handed it to one of the Delaware. The Delaware took it and was about to drink it when the bartender swept it from his hand. The glass fell to the floor and shattered.

Joe Stack reached across the bar and grabbed the bartender.

"Bubba!" the bartender shouted.

Bubba reached past the Delaware and put his hand on Stack's shoulder. It seemed that Big Bubba kept the peace in the settlement.

Stack was not a small man. He was easily six feet tall and might have weighed two hundred pounds, but he was dwarfed by Bubba.

"Oh Lord," Carson said, "Stack's gonna try him."

"He can't," Pike said, standing up. "Bubba will kill him."

He hurried to the bar and put his hand on Big Bubba's shoulder.

"Bubba," he said, urgently, hoping it would make a difference to the big man, "these men are all friends of mine."

Bubba looked down at Pike, frowning, understanding what he was saying.

"Your friends?"

"Yes."

Big Bubba looked at Joe Stack, still mulling it over in his head, and then took his huge hand off the man's shoulder.

"Your friends are my friends," Bubba said. He looked at the bartender and said, "Give them drinks."

"But Bubba—"

"Give 'em drinks!"

"All right, all right," the bartender said, and served the Delaware their drinks.

"No trouble," Bubba said to Pike.

"No trouble, Bubba," Pike agreed.

Stack looked at Pike, who smiled but got no smile in return.

"I could have handled it," Stack said, and looked away.

Pike doubted it, but said nothing. He returned to the table he was sharing with Carson.

"Ungrateful, isn't he?"

"Stack's okay, Pike," Carson said, "once you get to know him."

Pike looked over at Stack, who slumped over the bar, and said, "I guess I'll take your word for it."

CHAPTER TWO

Pike went looking for McConnell, but couldn't find him. That meant that his friend was probably with Gina. As much as mountain men disliked French Canadian men, they had nothing against the women. Following the fight, some of Pike's immediate celebrity spilled over on McConnell, and Skins had made it pay off—with Gina.

Pike had found himself the object of Angelique's interest. Angelique was as blond as Gina was dark, as busty as Gina was slim, as fiery as Gina was smoldering.

She had approached him later that same day of the fight . . .

Pike had decided that a more leisurely dip in the river might be good for his bruises, so he traveled downriver, stripped naked and waded into the water. While he was soaking he saw someone approaching, a blond woman wearing a simple brown dress that did her no justice. It was cheap, handmade, and strained to constrain her breasts and hips.

"Hello!" she called out.

"Hello!"

She sat down on the ground next to his clothes.

"Are you gonna sit there until I come out?" Pike asked.

She laughed and said, "But of course." Pike recognized a slight French accent.

"Why?"

"I saw you fight Bubba," she said. "I saw you beat Bubba. I wanted to see what kind of man could do that."

"A sore one."

"Do you hurt?"

"Yes," he said, "I do."

"Come out of the water," she said. "I can fix that."

"You can?"

"Yes, I can."

Pike assumed that she had been excited by the fight, and had sought him out because he was the victor.

"Will you come out," she asked, "or must I come in?"

Now he laughed and called out, "I'd like to see you come in."

She smiled, stood up and peeled off her dress. Her breasts were round, pale globes with pink nipples. They were firm, as were her thighs and buttocks. If she wasn't careful, she would grow plump and then fat, but at that moment she was every man's dream of what a woman should be, as she stepped into the water and moved toward him.

"Where does it hurt?" she asked.

"All over."

She came up to him and put her hands on his chest, then moved around behind him.

"Crouch down," she said, and he did. She put her hands on his shoulders and started kneading

25

his muscles.

"Is that better?" she asked.

"Much," he said, and it was.

She continued to massage his shoulders, his arms, his lower back, and then suddenly she reached around in front of him. His penis had swollen beneath the water, long and hard, and as she took hold of it he felt her wet, slippery breasts press into his back.

"Does this hurt?" she asked.

"No."

She slid her hand up and down the length of him and said, "Then perhaps I should stop?"

He shuddered from pleasure and said, "Oh, no . . ."

He brought her around in front of him and right there in the water, where anyone could have discovered them, he cupped her firm buttocks and lifted her onto him. As he slid inside of her she moaned and wrapped her strong legs around him. She bounced up and down on him so hard they created white water all around them, and he forgot all his aches and pains.

Later that evening she had taken him to her bed, and made her confession.

"Watching you fight Bubba," she said, "I just got all hot and itchy between my legs."

"Really?" he asked. "Are you hot and itchy now?"

"Oh, yes . . . ," she said, spreading her legs for him.

He slid his hand between her legs and rubbed her gently.

"Oh, all wet, too," he said. "Seems we should do something about that."

26

And they did . . . and again the next day.

Tonight he would tell her that he was leaving, and he was sure that she would make their last night together a memorable one. He was also sure she wouldn't get all clingy and weepy, because she wasn't that type of woman.

She worked in the trading post, but he avoided that at the moment. He wanted to find McConnell and tell him of Carson's invitation.

If he could pry Skins away from the charms of the dark Gina.

CHAPTER THREE

At that moment, in the tent that Pike shared with McConnell, Skins and Gina were very involved with each other.

Gina moaned and cried out with every stab of McConnell's cock, and McConnell groaned as he drove both of them toward orgasm.

Gina's body was so slender it was almost as if she had no breasts, but she had the largest nipples McConnell had ever seen. When they got big and hard as they were now, he felt as if someone were pressing two small stones against his chest.

He had his hands beneath her, cupping her slim, almost boyish buttocks, and her long, lean legs were wrapped around his waist.

She urged him on in French, a language he had absolutely no grasp of, but he knew that when she cried out, *"Oui, oui,"* it meant, "yes, yes," and he kept going.

Neither of the cots would accommodate them, so they had spread a couple of blankets on the floor of the tent. The hardness of the floor meant there was no give beneath them, and when he drove himself into her he achieved maximum penetration every time.

Earlier, before they had reached this point of mindlessness, Gina wished she had a soft mattress as her friend Angelique did. Now all she wished was that Skins McConnell would *never* stop what he was doing.

Pike and McConnell enjoyed privacy, so they had pitched their tent away from the settlement, where there was less chance that they would be bothered. As Pike approached the tent now, the sounds that came from within were unmistakable. He stopped and listened for a moment, but McConnell and Gina sounded so caught up in each other that he knew if he listened any further he'd have to go and hunt up Angelique to take care of his own needs.

As he turned to leave, he heard something from his left, and turned just in time to ward off the blow with his arm. One man had charged him, holding a large piece of dead wood as a club. The blow stung his arm, but he still had feeling in it. As Pike backed away from the next wild swing, he banged into the man who had been charging from the right. He and that man went down in a heap.

As Pike righted himself and gained his feet, he saw that there were three of them, and that they were all similarly armed with clubs. Pike's Hawken and Kentucky Pistol were in the tent, and all he had on him was his knife. He took it out and waited as the three men decided what they wanted to do.

"Put the knife away, Pike," one of the men said. "We was only told to rough you up some."

"You want to rough me up, you come ahead," Pike said, "but you're gonna take a chance on getting cut."

The man who spoke said, "All right, if you want it

that way." He threw his club down and took out his own knife.

One of the other men said, "I ain't getting paid enough to kill or be killed, Lavery." That man threw down his club and walked off. Seconds later the second man followed. That left just Pike and the man called Lavery, facing each other with knives drawn.

"All right," Lavery said, "let me by and we'll forget this."

"I ain't forgetting nothing," Pike said. "Who hired you to do this?"

"I said let me by!" Lavery shouted.

"Not until you tell me who hired you."

"I can't do that."

"Talk, or we're gonna go at it."

Lavery was not as tall as Pike, and he was giving away some fifty pounds. He must have known how Pike felt facing Big Bubba.

"Come on, Lavery," Pike said. "Make up your mind. I got things to do, and killing you is not something I want to spend a lot of time doing."

Lavery was licking his lips nervously, the knife in his hand wavering, his eyes darting from side to side, looking for a way to escape.

"All right," he said, finally, "it was Comfort. He wanted us to bang you up some because of what you did to him. Now let me by!"

"Comfort," Pike said, without surprise. "All right, Lavery. Give Comfort a message for me."

"What?"

"Tell him next time he wants some dirty work done, do it himself."

Pike stepped aside and Lavery moved by him warily, then started running. It had been a situation where Pike felt someone was going to die.

He was glad it hadn't turned out that way.

He was about to walk away himself when suddenly, from inside the tent, a woman's high-pitched wail cut through the air, and then a man groaned like a wounded bull.

Pike put his knife away, said, "Well, it sounds like *someone's* dying," and approached the tent.

CHAPTER FOUR

Pike moved to the front of the tent, figuring from the last sounds he'd heard that McConnell and Gina must have finished doing what they were doing.

"Skins?"

He heard people moving around inside, and then heard McConnell curse. A few moments later McConnell came out, wearing only his pants, and favoring his left foot.

"What happened to you?" Pike asked.

"I stubbed my damn toe," McConnell said, irritably. "What the hell do you want?"

"Oh, I'm sorry," Pike said with exaggerated politeness. "Did I interrupt something? From the sound of things I thought you were finished."

"You were listening?"

"I came to talk to you," Pike said. "When I heard what was going on inside I figured you must be having a fight, or else you and Gina were . . ."

"Well, we were."

"That explains why you didn't help me."

"Help you what?"

"Comfort sent three of his friends to beat my brains out with clubs."

"You look like you still got your brains."

"They didn't want to go up against a knife with clubs," Pike explained, "and they hadn't been paid enough to use their own knives. Luckily, while we're in the settlement, we had all left our guns somewhere else."

"Well, I'm sorry I didn't hear anything," McConnell said, rubbing his hand over his hair. "Jesus, it's cold."

"Are you finished in there?"

"Uh, oh, yeah, I'm done."

"Get yourself dressed then and I'll buy you a drink. I've also got something to ask you."

"Okay," McConnell said, "I'll get dressed and I'll meet you at the saloon."

"Okay," Pike said. "Don't go in there and get distracted again."

"I think I'm done," McConnell said.

"Yeah, well," Pike said, "tell that to Gina."

Pike waved and McConnell went back inside.

On the way back to the saloon tent Pike decided not to make a point of confronting Comfort. The man had already paid a heavy price with a jaw that might be broken, but he also didn't know how his new friendship with Bubba would stand up to the big man's relationship with Comfort.

Better to stay out of their way until they pulled up stakes tomorrow morning.

"Comanche country?" Skins McConnell asked over his beer.

"That's what he said."

"What do you think?" McConnell asked.

"It's an interesting idea," Pike said. "We could get some heavy buffalo hunting done down there."

"Yeah, but we've never been down there."

"Carson has," Pike said, "and he's got a fella with him, Joe Stack, who was married to a Comanche woman, and he's got three Delaware Indians with him."

McConnell rubbed his jaw and said, "Comanche Indians can smell Delaware Indians."

"I know it."

"And you still want to go?"

"Not if you don't," Pike said. "We've both got to agree on this."

"Well," McConnell said, "why not? It'll be a new experience. Tell Carson we'll go. When is he going to be ready to leave?"

"Same as us," Pike said. "Tomorrow morning."

"All right," McConnell said, "I'll see about the supplies."

"And I'll talk to Carson."

McConnell stood up and Pike said, "Where are you gonna be after you buy the supplies?"

"Where else?" McConnell said. "I'll be saying goodbye to Gina."

"You got enough strength left?"

"I'll find it somewhere," McConnell said with a leer. "What about you and Angelique? Gonna say goodbye?"

"Of course," Pike said. "I couldn't leave without saying goodbye. That just wouldn't be polite."

McConnell started out and passed Carson on the way in, greeting him in passing.

Carson went over and sat with Pike.

"So? What's the verdict?"

"You got two more for your party, Kit, if you still want us."

"That's great! We'll have us a fine hunt, Pike. We haven't been buffalo hunting together in a long time.

34

How many animals you got?"

"We've got four mules."

"And we've got eight," Carson said. "We'll lead two each, and Stack will ride point."

"Sounds good, Kit."

"Time for a beer?"

"I got time," Pike said. He wasn't going to go and see Angelique until it got dark.

Over in a corner Comfort sat and smoldered, staring across the floor at Jack Pike. Comfort was even more upset that the three men he'd sent after Pike had failed.

But he wasn't finished yet.

Not by a long sight.

CHAPTER FIVE

Pike went to Angelique's private tent later that evening, after he felt she had closed up her trading post—she not only worked there, she owned the place—and done whatever it was she had to do afterward—taking inventory, or whatever.

He left Carson sitting alone in the saloon tent, telling him he had a "previous engagement."

"Female?"

"None of your business," Pike said, good-naturedly. "Female," he said, with a nod.

Stack was at the bar, drinking as he had been all day—"He can handle it," Kit Carson assured him— and Pike didn't know where the three Delaware Indians were.

He assumed that Skins McConnell was saying goodbye to Gina.

Which is what he was about to start doing to—and with—Angelique.

"Angelique?"

He was standing outside her private tent, which was right behind the trading post, the only wooden structure in the settlement.

"Pike?"

"That's me."

"Come on in."

Pike lifted the flap and entered. There was a single candle lit, and Angelique was standing in the center of the tent, naked. Her big, round breasts were covered with goose flesh, and her nipples were already hard. She was rubbing her hands along her smooth, fleshy thighs.

"I thought I'd save us some time," Angelique said. "Since we are going to spend the night saying goodbye I didn't want to waste any of it."

His hands immediately went to work on his shirt and he said, "Good thinking."

Angelique's tent was the largest in the settlement. It had to be to accommodate her four poster bed, together with down mattress.

When they were both naked they met in a long embrace, and then moved to the bed together. The springs protested when they sank onto the bed together, but neither of them noticed.

"Do you say goodbye quickly," she asked him, lying atop him, "or slowly?"

"Well," he said, "I move around a lot, which means I've had a lot of practice saying goodbye in many different ways."

"Oh, really?" she asked, running her forefinger over his lips.

He slid his hands down her back until he was rubbing his palms over her buttocks. Slowly, he began to knead them, every so often running one finger along the crease between them.

"Mmmm," she said, kissing his chest, licking his nipples.

She kissed his neck, his chin and then his mouth,

pushing her tongue past his lips. She lifted her hips so that the head of his cock was poking at her moist portal, and then she made a quick motion and engulfed him.

"Oh, yes," she said, sitting up on him and stretching her hands up over her head. Her breasts lifted with the movement, and he reached up to cup them and tweak the nipples. He felt her shudder with orgasm immediately, a small one that made her moan and smile.

"Oh, this is going to be a very special night," she said.

He couldn't have agreed with her more.

She began to ride him up and down, slowly at first, and then faster. The candlelight cast flickering shadows on her body as she moved, and Pike just lay there and let her do the work. She was so absolutely beautiful in that light, undulating and swiveling and moving over him, that he was too stunned to do much more than watch her—for a while. Pretty soon it became impossible *not* to move and he began matching her moves with his hips. Finally, he reached for her, took her by the hips and rolled over so that he was on top of her.

Now he was moving over her, driving himself into her as far as he could go, and she was whimpering and whispering his name over and over.

They were driving toward a shattering climax when suddenly there was a draft in the room, as if someone had lifted the tent flap.

Someone had.

Pike looked over his shoulder and saw Comfort standing there holding a pistol on him, with two men standing behind him.

Pike recognized the two men behind Comfort as being two of the three who had attacked him previously.

"Did you pay them enough this time?" he asked.

The two men showed him their pistols too and one of them said, "He paid enough."

"Oh, Pike!" Angelique cried out, so near her completion that she didn't realize what was going on, only that she was so close.

"Go ahead and finish her," Comfort said, through clenched teeth. "We'll wait."

Pike didn't see any other option. Besides, it would give him some time to think. He looked down at Angelique, who was still oblivious to the situation, and began to move again.

CHAPTER SIX

"All right," Comfort said, "stand up."

It was obviously painful for him to speak, but he must have thought that the outcome would be worth the pain.

Pike moved off Angelique and stood up. Angelique quickly took stock of the situation—now that she was in full possession of her faculties again—and said, "Boys, this is a private party."

"We just made it a fivesome," Comfort said.

Pike could see the men behind Comfort ogling Angelique's opulent curves. For her part, she didn't seem frightened of them, and made no effort to cover her nakedness.

"All right, boys," Comfort said, "she's all yours." He pointed his pistol directly at Pike's face and said, "And you're going to watch."

"Well," Angelique said, sitting up, "I hope they're good."

"Don't worry, lady," one of them said, "you won't be disappointed."

He and his friend put their pistols down and began to lower their pants. When their pants were down about halfway, Angelique's hand came up from beneath her mattress with a pistol and she fired at one of them. The ball struck him in the head and he fell backward.

Comfort turned his head in shock and Pike was on him. He grabbed the pistol from his hand and hit him in the jaw. Comfort went down, the pain in his already wounded jaw so intense he started to cry.

The third man made a grab for his pistol but tripped on his lowered pants. From his chest he eyed the pistol, which was still within his reach.

"Don't try it!" Pike called out.

The man looked at Pike and Pike said, "I'm willing to kill you, and I'm not even getting paid for it."

The man believed him, and gave up on the gun.

Pike looked down at Comfort, who was still crying. He was holding both hands to his mouth and blood was seeping through his fingers. Somehow, Pike could not bring himself to feel sorry for the man.

From outside they heard footsteps as people approached on the run, in response to the shot.

"Cover up, Angelique," Pike said. "We're about to have lots of company."

She pulled the sheet around her and said, "I thought we already did."

After the mess was cleaned up and Comfort and his men were dragged away, Pike sat on the bed next to Angelique and picked up her pistol.

"Where did this come from?" he asked.

"I always keep it under my mattress," she said. "A girl like me can't be too careful."

"And what kind of girl are you?"

She had wrapped herself in her sheet when the men came in to remove Comfort and his friends, and now

41

she uncovered herself, like a flower that was blooming right in front of his eyes.

"This kind," she said, cupping her breasts and lifting them to him.

"After what happened you're still . . . ready?"

"With you, Pike," she said, taking the empty gun from his hand and dropping it to the floor, "I'm always ready."

Pike lay down with her again, and for a fleeting moment he wondered if they shouldn't reload the pistol—but just for a moment.

In the morning Pike and McConnell saddled their horses and led their mules over in front of the trading post. They found Kit Carson, Joe Stack, and the three Delaware waiting, mounted and leading their mules.

Also waiting, on the steps of the trading post, were Angelique and Gina.

Pike and McConnell rode over and looked down at the girls. Gina walked over to McConnell while Angelique stayed on the steps and smiled up at Pike.

"Three days is a short time together," Angelique said to him.

"I know."

"Will you be back this way?"

"It's possible."

"No promises," she said, and her smile turned sad.

"No promises."

"Well, I will be here."

He reached over and she held his hand in both of hers, briefly.

"Are you two lovers ready?" Kit Carson asked.

Pike looked over at Skins McConnell, who had just leaned over and kissed Gina goodbye.

"Yeah," he said, "we're ready."

PART TWO

COMANCHE
COUNTRY

CHAPTER SEVEN

It was necessary for the six hunters to cross the desolate Cimarron to get to the country they wanted to hunt in. Mountain men were notorious for refusing to carry water canteens or skins on their saddles. They usually felt that if they needed water they could ride to it.

With Joe Stack along, they felt even more certain that they'd be able to find water when they needed it.

It would have struck anyone watching them as odd that the Delaware were dressed like white men, in buckskins, while Joe Stack, a white man, was wearing only a red G-string. Pike had spent many hours in the saddle over the years, but he could not imagine riding with his bare buttocks slapping the saddle, the way Joe Stack was.

Stack rode faster and farther ahead of the rest of them, because Kit Carson, Pike and the others were each leading two mules.

They were riding across the bare prairie, not a tree, rock or bush in sight. To their left were the mountains, vague and seeming to waver in the heat. In fact it seemed as if a wavering blanket spread out before them as the heat reflected off the hard ground.

"His ass must be sunburned by now," Skins McConnell said about Stack.

"I think his ass is used to it," Pike said.

"He talks even less than the Delaware do."

"According to Kit, he really knows this country well. As long as he can get us where we want to go, I don't care if he *never* speaks."

"What's that?" McConnell said, looking up ahead.

Pike squinted and said, "Looks like Stack is coming back."

"He just left."

"Maybe he found something."

Kit Carson was riding in the lead and when he saw Stack returning he called the column to a stop. Pike handed the reins of his mules to McConnell.

"I'll see what's going on."

He rode up to stand next to Carson as Joe Stack approached.

"What's wrong, Joe?" Carson asked.

"There's a body up ahead," Stack said.

"A body?" Pike asked.

Stack continued to talk to Carson.

"It's a woman, possibly an Indian."

"Comanche?" Carson asked.

"I can't tell from here."

"Did you get close to her?" Pike asked.

"No."

"Why not?"

"It could be a trap."

"A trap?"

"The Comanche could have staked her out there to draw us to her," Carson explained to Pike.

"How do we find out if that's true or not?"

"That's up to Joe. Joe?" Carson said.

"We can bypass her," Stack said.

"If she's hurt, or even stranded, she'll need our

help, or she'll die," Pike said.

Stack kept staring at Carson.

"Check it out, Joe," Carson said. "We'll slow our pace."

For the first time Stack looked at Pike, and he didn't look like a happy man.

"All right," he said, finally.

Stack wheeled his horse around and headed out again.

"What's his problem?" Pike asked.

"He doesn't like white men very much."

"You're white."

Carson smiled.

"He doesn't believe it."

"Hell," Pike said, "*he's* white!"

"He was born white," Carson said, "but he's more Comanche than anything else."

"Will he fight them if we run up against them?"

"He wouldn't have, while his wife was alive, but she's dead now."

"How did she die?"

"She was killed," Carson said, "by a Comanche. Come on, let's move."

They moved forward at a reduced pace, waiting for Stack to finish his scouting and return. Pike wondered why the Comanche would strand one of their women out here in the desert if it *wasn't* a trap.

"What do you think?" McConnell asked.

"I don't know what to think," Pike said. "This isn't my kind of country."

"It's hot, isn't it?"

"Yeah," Pike said. "I think I prefer snow."

"Maybe we'll get used to it."

"Sure," Pike said, but he was wondering how

47

anyone could get used to heat this oppressive.

He looked up when he hard Carson call out for them to stop.

"He's coming back," McConnell said, and reached for Pike's reins.

He was waiting with Carson when Stack reached them.

"Well?" Carson asked Stack.

"No trap," Stack said.

"Are you sure?" Pike asked. "I mean, they could be hiding."

Stack looked at Pike and asked, "Where?"

Pike looked around them and as far as he could see, he saw . . . nothing.

"How much farther ahead is she?" Carson asked.

"Maybe a mile."

"Is she alive?"

"Yes."

"Is she moving?"

"Yes, she's walking."

"All right," Carson said, "stay with us until we reach her, and then you can ride up ahead."

Stack nodded and fell in next to Carson. Pike went back and retrieved his mule reins from McConnell.

"Well?"

"We're about to pick up a passenger."

Pike saw her, and knew that Carson and Stack must have spotted her before he did.

Several moments later McConnell said, "I see her."

"Yeah," Pike said.

They approached her slowly, so as not to spook her. She turned once, saw them coming, and then fell to the ground. She just sat there, waiting for them.

As they got close to her Pike saw that she was young. Closer yet and he could see that she was extremely pretty. The look on her face was defiant, but he knew she must have been scared. She had no idea whether they were there to save her or . . . or what?

When they reached her, Carson dismounted, and Stack stayed on his horse. Pike handed his reins to McConnell again and dismounted. He walked over to where Carson was standing, looking down at her.

"Comanche?" he asked.

"Look at her."

Pike looked at the girl again and saw it.

"She's Crow."

"Yes."

"What the hell is she doing out here?"

"I guess maybe we should try and find out," Carson said. "How good is your Crow?"

"Not as good as yours."

"All right."

Carson hunkered down next to the girl and talked to her. Some of it Pike was able to understand, and some of it he heard later from Carson.

"What is your name?" Carson asked.

"Walking Star."

"How did you come to be here?"

"I was taken from my people by whites. They used me, brought me here."

"And what happened?"

"They were killed by the Comanche."

"And you?"

"They said they would not kill me," she said. "They left me out here."

Carson studied her, then stood up and relayed what had been said to Pike.

"I think they want to see if she can survive," Carson said.

"Which means what?"

"They'll be coming back to check on her."

49

"That means we'd better get moving."

"Right. We'll have to put her on one of the mules and move the supplies to the others."

"That'll take too long," Pike said. "She can ride with me."

"All right," Carson said, nodding. He spoke to her, indicating Pike, and then back to his own horse.

Pike moved closer to her and extended his hand.

"You're a real beauty, aren't you?"

Slowly, she reached her hand out so that he could grasp it, and he pulled her to her feet.

"Come on," he said, taking her to his horse. He mounted first, and then lifted her up behind him. She put her arms around his waist and pressed herself tightly against his back.

"Wherever we go," McConnell said, shaking his head, "you always manage to find a girl."

CHAPTER EIGHT

They camped the first night by a small water hole Joe Stack led them to, unerringly.

"Even if he didn't know where they were," Kit Carson told Pike, "he can smell water."

One of the Delaware Indians did the cooking, and turned out to be a really good cook. The other two took care of the animals.

Pike, Carson and McConnell sat around the fire together on one side. On the other side the three Delaware Indians sat. Joe Stack had found himself a space somewhere.

The Crow girl, Walking Star, sat behind Pike. Since she had ridden with him most of the day, she seemed to have latched onto him and followed him wherever he went.

"Looks like you might have trouble getting rid of her now," Carson said.

Pike looked behind him, where Walking Star sat eating. She returned his gaze without expression. She had the eyes of a doe, large and liquid, and at times she even looked startled.

"What are we gonna do with her?" Pike asked.

"Seems that would be up to you," Skins McConnell said.

"Why me?"

"You're the one she likes."

"Well," Pike said, "we can leave her at the first town we come to."

"With the whites?" Carson said. "They'd either turn her out, or make a slave out of her."

"Might be better than what the Comanches would do to her," Pike said.

"I don't know about that," Kit Carson said. "If they wanted her dead they would have killed her."

"They left her out here by herself," McConnell said. "If that ain't the same as killing her . . ."

"It may have been a test," Carson said.

"Comanche don't like the Crow any more than they like the Delaware," Pike pointed out.

"Look at her, Pike," Carson said. "She's just about the prettiest squaw I ever seen, Comanche, Crow *or* Delaware. After all, a man is a man."

"You're saying some Comanche wanted her and decided to test her?" McConnell said.

"I'm saying maybe."

"That means that they'll come looking for her," McConnell said, "and *that* means that the sooner we shuck her the better."

"We can't just dump her," Pike said, looking over his shoulder at her. "She *is* mighty pretty."

"You want to keep her for your own?" McConnell asked.

"I didn't say that," Pike said.

"Then what *are* you saying?"

Pike gave McConnell an annoyed look and said, "I don't *know* what I'm saying!"

McConnell looked at Carson and said, "Well, at least some things ain't changed."

Pike handed his plate to McConnell and said, "Here, make yourself useful and clean up. I'm go-

52

ing to check on the horses."

Pike stood up and started away from the fire. Walking Star also rose and followed.

He turned and said, "Stay here."

He started to walk again, and she followed.

"Stay here!"

He walked, she followed.

"Oh, for Chrissake!" he said.

He looked at Carson and McConnell, and they studiously avoided his eyes, but he could tell they were laughing.

He walked toward the horses at a swift pace. Let her follow if she wanted to.

The Delaware had done a good job of picketing the horses, as he'd already known. He went to his own horse, bent and checked his legs and the bottom of his hooves. He wanted to make sure he was sound. Out here if your horse went lame you would really be up the creek . . . so to speak.

When he turned away he literally bumped into Walking Star. He had to reach out and grab her so she wouldn't fall over.

"Don't get so close next time," he said, releasing her.

For the first time she smiled at him, and he saw how truly pretty she was.

"I make you good squaw," she said, in English.

He stared at her, dumbfounded.

"You speak English!" he finally said.

"Yes," she said, "I speak English good."

"Well, why didn't you tell us?"

"I not want you to know, yet," she said. "I listen to what you say."

"And if you didn't like what we were saying?"

"I run away," she said. "I not let you give me to the Comanche."

"I'm not going to give you to the Comanche," he said.

"I know," she said. "You keep me for yourself."

"I can't keep you, Walking Star."

"You keep me," she said, again. "I stay with you."

"Look—" he said, but she was staring at him with those big, sad, doe eyes and he stopped. "How did you get out here?"

"White man buy me from my people, keep me since I small."

"How many years?"

She stared at him and he said, "Four years, five years? Six years?"

"Six year," she said.

He guessed she was about nineteen, which meant that her people had sold her when she was about thirteen.

"And he was killed by the Comanche?"

She nodded, and said, "Five days ago."

"You've been out here for five days?"

"Yes."

"Then you were surviving pretty well when we came along."

"Much better now," she said, smiling.

"Why didn't the Comanche kill you?"

"All braves use me," she said, "and after, one brave want me."

"You mean they all . . . raped you?"

"They all use me," she said, nodding.

"And one man decided he wanted to keep you?"

"Yes."

"What happened?"

"Others say kill me," she explained. "He say no, he test me, see if I make good squaw."

"So they left you out here to see if you would survive."

She nodded.

"How long were they going to leave you here?"

"Seven days."

"So they'll be looking for you in two. Maybe we'll put enough space between us and them by then."

But he knew that wouldn't be true. They were leading eight mules, and they'd stopped to hunt the first chance they got. If the Comanche wanted her badly enough, and followed their trail, they'd catch up soon enough.

"How many braves in the party that killed your man?"

"Eleven, maybe twelve."

Two-to-one odds, unless they returned with more.

"All right," he said, "we'd better get some sleep."

He led her back to the fire and made a place for her to sleep, then relayed his conversation to Carson and McConnell.

"So, she speaks English, huh?" McConnell said. "Sneaky little devil."

"She wanted to hear what we were saying before she let us know."

"Smart," Carson said. "So, what do we do with her?"

Pike shrugged.

"Let her travel with us, I guess, until we decide."

"Well, let's get some sleep, then," Carson said. "I want to get an early start in the morning."

They set up a three-man watch with the three Delaware, but Joe Stack said he'd take one, making it a four-man watch.

Pike settled down on his blanket to sleep, but before long he felt Walking Star lie down behind him with her blanket. She wrapped it around both of

55

them and pressed herself so tightly against him that he could feel the heat of her body. He felt his groin tighten in reaction and there was nothing he could do about it.

"I sleep with you," she said into his ear, and he didn't argue.

Once during the night Pike awoke, not on his own, but because something had awakened him. He looked around and saw Joe Stack sitting with his back to the fire. When you were standing watch you had to be careful not to look into the fire, because it destroyed your night vision.

Stack was sitting perfectly still, so it wasn't he who had awakened Pike. He put his head back down again, conscious of Walking Star's weight against his back.

And then he heard it—or rather, felt it. A shudder ran through her body, and he thought he heard a small sob.

She was crying, and it had awakened him.

He turned over so that he was facing her and looked at her face. There were tears wetting her cheeks, but she was still asleep.

"Shhh," he said to her. He put his arms around her and kissed her forehead. She snuggled closer to him and he could feel her breath on his chin, feel her breasts beneath the deerskin dress she was wearing.

She became calm and stopped crying, sleeping peacefullly now.

With her face and body pressed close to him like that, he was anything but peaceful and calm.

CHAPTER NINE

Pike awoke the next morning to the smell of coffee and bacon. He sat up, assuming that one of the Delaware was making coffee. Suddenly he became aware that Walking Star was not on the blanket with him. He looked around, wondering if she had run away for some reason, but then he saw her at the fire.

It was she who was preparing breakfast.

The three Delaware were awake, but they were sitting away from the fire—away from Walking Star.

Pike went to the fire and said, "Good morning."

She smiled at him, poured a cup of coffee and handed it to him.

"Where did you learn how to make coffee?" he asked. It was not something that Indians were known for drinking. In fact, he had never even known an Indian who *liked* drinking it.

"You forget I live with a white man for six years."

"That's right," he said, "I did forget."

He looked around, saw that Kit Carson was up and gone, as was Stack. McConnell was still asleep.

"Where are the others?"

"They go scouting," she said.

Pike looked over at the Delaware.

"Did they eat?"

She shook her head.

"They will not eat what I cook."

Pike looked over at the Delaware and saw that they were chewing on some dried meat. He shrugged. What they wanted to eat was their business.

He walked over to McConnell and nudged him with his foot.

"Skins! Time to get up!"

From the looks of the sky, he figured the sun had been up only about half an hour. Plenty of time to eat breakfast and get an early start.

He carried the cup of coffee with him to the water, which he splashed onto his face to wake himself up. When he returned to the fire, McConnell was sitting there eating breakfast.

"She's a better cook than that Delaware," McConnell said.

"Maybe she'll do the cooking from now on," Pike said.

"I cook," she said, grinning happily.

"Well," McConnell said, "I guess that's settled."

At that moment Kit Carson and Joe Stack reappeared.

"You can smell that bacon and coffee a mile off," Carson said.

"It's delicious," McConnell said.

"Maybe so," Carson said, "but if we can smell it a mile off, the Comanche can smell it ten miles off."

"Well, too late to do anything about it now," Pike said.

"Except eat it," McConnell said.

"You've got a point there," Carson said. He hunkered down and took the plate and cup Walking

58

Star offered him.

"Thank you, Walking Star."

Joe Stack walked away, making it plain that he didn't want to eat. Pike didn't know if that was because the girl had cooked, or he simply wasn't hungry.

Stack went över to the Delaware, spoke to them briefly, and then they went to saddle the horses and ready the mules.

After breakfast Walking Star cleaned the plates and utensils in the water and put them away. One of the Delaware came over, took them and stowed them away on one of the mules.

Pike went to his horse and checked his saddle, cinching it even tighter. McConnell was doing the same. They usually liked to saddle their own animals, and when they didn't they at least checked them. Walking Star stood aside, watching Pike carefully.

"Okay, we ready?" Carson asked, coming up behind Pike and McConnell.

"We're ready," Pike said. "Kit, the Delaware seem to resent Walking Star."

"That's their problem," Carson said. "They were hired to do a job, and they'll do it."

If Carson was satisfied, then so was Pike.

Carson mounted up and said, "By midday we should be encountering some buffalo."

"Well, good," Pike said. "After all, that's what we came here for."

"Amen," McConnell said.

Pike mounted up, reached down for Walking Star and pulled her up to sit behind him. This time when she flattened herself against him she turned her face so that her cheek was pressed to him.

59

He wondered briefly about her rising early to cook coffee and bacon, two items that had an aroma that would travel for miles, then decided that she had simply done it to please him, and not to give their location to the Comanche.

She couldn't be that devious.

CHAPTER TEN

The brave called Hawk Moon sniffed at the air, separating all the scents he was picking up.

"White man's camp," he said, looking over at his leader, Strong Elk.

"I smell it," Strong Elk said.

He-Who-Takes-Many-Scalps leaned over and said, "We take them?"

"We will take them," Strong Elk said. "There is no hurry."

"You are thinking of the Crow woman," Hawk Moon said. "My brothers, it would have been better to kill her."

"She may be dead even now," Strong Elk said. "If she is not, I want her."

"We can get her today, and ride on the whites," He-Who-Takes-Many-Scalps said.

"She has one more day," Strong Elk said. "Tomorrow, we ride for her. After that, we take the white men."

"They will kill many buffalo before then," Hawk Moon said.

"And they will pay for each one they kill," Strong Elk said. "Come, we must meet Two-Faces and the rest of the braves at the appointed place."

He wheeled his pony around and the other eleven braves followed him.

Behind his back Hawk Moon and He-Who-Takes-Many-Scalps exchanged a glance that said they thought their leader was wrong. In spite of that however, they would follow him because he was their leader—and their friend—and they were loyal to him.

Even when they thought he was wrong.

CHAPTER ELEVEN

The land was different here.

There were trees, and hills and valleys, and there was sign for Joe Stack to read. In the distance, to their right, there were still mountains.

"There is a herd up ahead," he announced.

"How far?" Carson asked.

"A few miles, maybe."

Carson looked at the others and said, "We should be getting ourselves some beef real soon now, boys." He grinned at Pike and said, "I sure hope we brought along enough mules to carry all the hides."

Pike grinned back.

"There they are," Stack said.

The others saw them at the same time. They were atop a high rise, and the herd was at the bottom, in a basin-like depression.

"What a set-up," Carson said. "We can sit up here and pick them off."

"Where's the sport in that?" McConnell asked.

"Skins," Carson said, "we're not here for sport; we're here for money."

"He's got a point," Pike said.

"Well, all right," Carson said, "let's get set up."

63

They took down their rifles and powder horns and everything else they needed to be able to load and reload quickly. Once they started firing, the buffalo would start to move, and they would need to reload quickly to get off several shots each.

Pike noticed that Carson had brought along two rifles, as had Stack. The Delaware wouldn't be firing; they'd be reloading for Carson and Stack.

The way things were finally set up, the third Delaware reloaded for McConnell while McConnell used the Delaware's rifle for his second shot.

That left Pike to reload for himself.

"I will reload," Walking Star said.

"You know how to load a rifle?"

"You forget—" she said.

"I know, you lived with a white man for six years."

Pike took one of the other Delaware's rifles, so that he'd have one to fire while Walking Star was reloading his.

"All right," Carson said, "fire!"

Carson, Pike and McConnell sighted and fired and then handed the rifle behind them, accepting the second rifle in the same motion. They sighted and fired and then reached back. Pike's rifle was ready first, which he didn't realize until after they were finished. The herd had run off, leaving behind their fallen brothers.

"How many?" McConnell asked.

"Four," Carson said. "No misses."

"I got three," McConnell said. "One miss."

They looked at Pike who said, "Uh, six . . . no misses."

"Six?" McConnell asked.

Pike was as puzzled as they were. He'd assumed that they would all have fired the same number of times.

"Uh, Walking Star was reloading for me," he said, as if that explained it.

They all looked at her and she smiled.

"I load good."

"You load very good," Pike said, "and fast."

"I'll say she does," Carson said.

The three Delaware exchanged glances, then took their knives and tramped down the hill to begin skinning.

"They don't look too happy," Pike said.

"Would you be," McConnell asked, "if a woman had put you to shame?"

"And a Crow woman, to boot," Carson said.

"Come on," Pike said, "let's take care of those skins."

"Bring back some meat," Walking Star said, "and I will cook it."

"That's the best offer I've heard all day," Kit Carson said.

They spent the afternoon skinning the kill, and then sent two of the Delaware up the hill for a couple of mules to carry the skins back up to camp.

Kit butchered one of the buffalo for the meat, took it to Walking Star, and she cooked it for their dinner. The Delaware, however, insisted on eating their dried meat, and stayed away from the fire.

Joe Stack, however, partook of the cooked beef. It was a good sign that he had started to accept Walking Star as part of their party. Pike suspected that it was more for her ability loading than cooking.

"In the morning," Carson said, "we can track the herd to their next stop. There are enough of them to make us rich men."

"Or at least reasonably well-off," Pike said. "I

mean, who really wants to be rich?"

They all exchanged glances, and then McConnell said, "I could stand to be."

"What could you do if you became truly wealthy?" Pike asked.

McConnell thought a moment and said, "I think I'd find me the world's longest poker game."

"What about you, Kit?"

"I don't know," Carson said. "I think maybe I'd travel."

"Around the country?" McConnell asked.

"More, around the world. Just think about all the places there are that you've never seen."

"Too many for me to see in one lifetime," McConnell said. "I usually don't leave the mountains."

"And what about you?" Carson asked Pike. "What would you do if you became rich?"

Pike took the time to pour himself another cup of coffee before answering.

Finally, he said, "I'd buy me a mountain."

"A mountain?" Carson asked.

"My own mountain," Pike said. "I'd stock it with game, and I don't think I'd ever come down."

They all fell silent then, thinking about his answer, and then they were all surprised by who spoke next.

"That's what I'd do," Joe Stack said.

They all looked at him, studying him.

"Buy me a mountain," Stack said, nodding. "Yeah, that's what I'd do."

Pike noticed Stack staring at him, looking at him differently.

Without even trying, he had managed to gain the man's respect.

*　　*　　*

The next morning they rose early enough to keep Walking Star from putting on the coffee and bacon.

"We've got plenty of meat left from last night," Kit Carson said. "We can eat that."

"Fine," Pike said, and the others agreed. Even the Delaware decided to have some of the meat. They must have gotten tired of eating dried beef.

Stack was suddenly a little friendlier today, to both Walking Star and Pike. He accepted some meat from Walking Star and even said thank you. Then he sat down next to Pike to eat it.

"What you said last night," he said.

"What?"

"About buying a mountain."

"Oh, that," Pike said. "It's just something I think about once in a while."

"I've thought about it for a long time," Stack said.

"But you lived on the plains, Joe," Pike said. "Why would you want to live on a mountain?"

"To be alone," he said, "and to be closer to my wife."

"Your wife?"

Stack looked up at the sky then, and Pike realized what he meant.

Suddenly, he had increased respect for Joe Stack.

They moved on then, in search of the herd, leaving behind the carcasses of more than a dozen animals, all of which would eventually rot, or be foraged by other wild animals.

Pike, as he had always done after a hunt, wondered about the right and wrong of what they just done.

CHAPTER TWELVE

Strong Elk raised his hand to call his men to a halt. They all sat astride their ponies, looking down at the carcasses that dotted the landscape below them.

Strong Elk and his band had joined with his cousin, Two-Faces, and the twenty braves he had riding with him.

Strong Elk and Two-Faces sat side by side, with Hawk Moon and He-Who-Takes-Many-Scalps right behind them.

"Butchers," Two-Faces said.

Strong Elk nodded wordlessly.

"Leave five men behind to salvage what they can," Strong Elk finally said.

"We will need them when we catch up to the whites," Two-Faces said.

"We will be meeting the others farther on," Strong Elk said. "We will be many when we catch the whites, and we will make them pay for this butchery."

"How long?" Two-Faces said. "How long before the whites rid the plains of the buffalo forever—and then what will we live on?"

"When we catch the whites," Strong Elk said, "we will ask them."

CHAPTER THIRTEEN

Joe Stack rode ahead of the rest, tracking the herd and keeping an eye out for trouble. It seemed odd to all of them that they did not catch up to the herd the next day. The only thing that they could figure was that the herd had kept running until they had to stop from exhaustion.

"If that's the case," Carson said when they camped that night, "they should still be pretty winded when we catch up to them tomorrow, because they must have run all day."

Of course, it didn't help that they had to move even more slowly now that some of the mules were weighted down with skins.

The following morning they once more dined on left-over buffalo meat, which was starting to become gamy by now. That was one thing about the mountains, Pike thought. Meat lasted longer in the cold weather.

As they started after the herd that second morning, Pike wondered how far behind them the Comanche were, and if they would really come after Walking Star.

"You are thinking about Strong Elk?" Walking

Star asked from behind him.

"Strong Elk?" Pike asked. "Who is that?"

"The Comanche brave who wants me," she said. "He is a chief's son."

"That's great," Pike said. "Why didn't you tell me that before?"

He felt her shrug behind him.

"Would that make a difference?" she asked. "Are you afraid of Strong Elk?"

"I don't even know him," Pike said. He wondered if Joe Stack did. He'd ask him when he came back.

They camped in the afternoon, just to rest the animals, and Joe Stack came riding back to them.

On Stack's advice they made a pot of coffee.

"You can't hide from Comanche," Stack reasoned. It made sense.

Over coffee Pike sat next to Stack and said, "I want to ask you something, Joe."

"What?"

"Do you know a Comanche named Strong Elk?"

Stack was raising his coffee cup to his lips when Pike said the name, and he stopped short.

"You do know him, don't you?"

"I know him."

"Well?"

"Well enough," Stack said. "Why?"

"It's Strong Elk who Walking Star says wants her," Pike explained.

Stack nodded, and sipped his coffee.

"Does that sound likely?"

"Very likely."

"Will he stop?"

"Not if he wants her badly enough."

"Then we've got trouble?"

Stack nodded and said, "We have trouble."

"Glad we had this talk," Pike said, and moved away to sit next to Kit Carson.

"I thought I was getting somewhere with Stack."

"Why? What happened?"

"He suddenly got very quiet again."

"What did you say to him?"

"I told him that Walking Star says that the brave who's after her is named Strong Elk."

Kit Carson's coffee cup stopped short on the way to his mouth.

"Not you, too," Pike said.

"You said that name to Stack?"

"Yep. Why?"

"His wife."

"What about her?"

Carson looked at Pike and said, "Strong Elk is the brave who killed her."

CHAPTER FOURTEEN

"Want to tell me about it?"

Carson leaned over to look at Joe Stack, who was staring off into space.

"Well, I don't guess Joe's gonna tell you about it," Carson said.

"I don't think so."

Carson took a deep breath and poured another cup of coffee.

"I'll give you the short version," he said. "The Comanche found Stack hurt and took him in."

"Why?"

Carson shrugged.

"He don't know, so I don't," Carson said. "They must have seen something in him—does that really matter?"

"I guess not. Go on."

"Well, it fell to Little Fawn to nurse Joe back to health, and they fell in love, only she already had a suitor."

"Strong Elk."

Carson nodded.

"That's why Strong Elk killed her?"

"Well," Carson said, "she was killed by someone

who raped her."

"In other words," Pike said, "Stack doesn't *know* that Strong Elk killed her."

"Oh, he knows," Carson said.

"But nothing that could stand up in . . ." Pike started, then realized they were talking about Comanche.

". . . in court?"

"Yeah, yeah, I know," Pike said. "So what happened?"

"After Little Fawn . . . died, the Comanche drove Joe Stack out. Strong Elk convinced them that she wouldn't have been killed if they hadn't accepted Joe Stack into their midst."

"Why didn't they kill Stack then?"

"Little Fawn's father was a medicine man. Out of respect for the old man they didn't kill his son-in-law."

"Lucky for Stack."

"Unlucky for Strong Elk," Carson said. "If Joe Stack ever sees him again he's gonna kill him."

"Or die trying?"

"See?" Kit Carson said. "You're getting to know ol' Joe Stack already."

CHAPTER FIFTEEN

"Where's the nearest town?" Pike asked.

Carson said, "This is Comanche country, Pike. There is a fort nearby, I believe. Stack could tell you more accurately."

"Stack still isn't talking, much."

"Well, you hit him with a shock. Give him time to get over it."

They both scanned the area ahead of them for Stack.

"It's getting late," Pike said.

"Stack has to locate the herd," Carson said. "If it gets dark we'll just have to camp nearby and start shooting come morning."

"Let's keep moving," Pike said.

They had gone another half mile when Joe Stack came riding back.

"Did you find them?"

"Yes," Stack said, "but by the time we reach them it will be dark."

"All right," Carson said, "we'll camp—can we camp above them?"

"No," Stack said, "but we can camp upwind

of them."

"Good enough," Carson said.

They camped and allowed Walking Star to prepare coffee and beans, on which they dined with dried meat. Walking Star sat very close to Pike while she ate. Pike could feel the tension in her, and she was as skittish as a doe.

Later, while she was cleaning up, he hunkered down next to her to help.

"What's the matter?" he asked.

She looked at him, a reply ready on her lips, but then she bit it back.

"I am frightened."

"Of what?"

"Strong Elk is coming," she said, "and he will be coming with many braves."

"How do you know that?"

"He spoke of meeting with many of his people."

"You understand Comanche?"

She shook her head.

"He knew I spoke the white man's tongue, so he also spoke it—to me."

Pike frowned. It sounded as if Strong Elk were trying to impress her with his importance. That meant that the man had an ego. Of course, the fact that he had killed Joe Stack's wife while raping her—assuming, of course, that he had—was further proof of the existence of a great ego.

"If he comes, he comes," Pike said. "We'll deal with it when the time comes."

She took hold of his arm and said, "You will not give me to him?"

He smiled at her and said, "No, I will not give you

to him."

She smiled back and continued her task of cleaning up.

Pike moved to Carson and told him the way Walking Star felt.

"She must smell them," Carson said, and of course he wasn't speaking literally. What he meant was that Walking Star could "feel" the presence of Strong Elk and his people behind them.

"I think we should set two-man watches," Pike said.

"Good idea," Carson said. "In addition to watching for Comanche, one of us could keep an eye on the herd. It's always possible that they could move during the night."

"One of us with one of the Delaware?" Pike asked.

"Done."

Pike took the first watch, with the Delaware named Mantooth. The Delaware watched their back trail while Pike sat facing the herd. There was a three-quarter moon and every so often he could see some movement among them. He would wake Carson in three hours.

He had been on watch an hour when he heard something behind him. He turned quickly, his Kentucky Pistol in his hand.

It was Walking Star.

"What are you doing up?" he asked.

"I cannot sleep," she said.

She waited, watching him with those big brown eyes, and finally he said, "All right. Come sit beside me."

She smiled and sat next to him, close enough so that their thighs were touching. He could feel the heat of her right through his pants.

"I have come to a decision," she said, after they sat

76

silent for a few moments.

"Oh? And what's that?"

"When Strong Elk comes, I will go to him."

"Why?"

"I do not want you—and the others—to die because of me."

"If we die it won't be because of you."

"But, if I go to him—"

"He'll try and kill us, anyway," Pike said. "We're white men in his country, Walking Star. That is enough reason for him to kill us." Also the fact that Joe Stack was among them. "So don't be thinking about going to him. I told you before, I won't let him take you."

"I am sorry, then," she said, leaning her head against his arm. "I do not want to be the death of you."

"Don't be sorry," Pike said. "If I die it will be because of a decision I made, not you."

He shifted, moving his left arm up and around her shoulders. She snuggled closer happily, her hand resting on his thigh, rubbing him lightly. He bent and kissed her forehead. She lifted her face to look at him and he kissed her lips. She opened her mouth beneath his and the kiss—which was meant to comfort her—deepened into something else.

She moaned beneath his mouth and shifted her body around to face him. Her hand moved up his thigh and found the bulge of his erect penis. His right hand ran along her warm, firm thigh, then up to cup her left breast through her dress. She shifted her legs, moaning again, and then he broke the kiss.

"Walking Star," he said, "not here, not now."

"When?" she asked, closing her hand over him.

"Later . . ."

"Later," she said, putting her head against his

arm. "Later, in our blankets . . ."

He shifted his legs, trying to accommodate the erection in his pants. Before long she had fallen asleep against him.

He sat there, listening to her quiet breathing, and he couldn't help thinking about making love to her.

The chances were good that Strong Elk and his people would catch up to them tomorrow. If they did, they could overwhelm them.

There were worse ways of spending your last night than in the arms of a lovely woman.

Later he had to wake her so they could go and wake McConnell. Walking Star went to the blanket they would share, saying she would warm it for him. Mantooth went and woke one of the other Delaware, Jonesy.

McConnell came awake immediately and asked, "All quiet?"

"The herd's been moving around some, but they haven't shifted."

"Good. What about the Comanche?"

"No sign that I know of."

"Good," he said again. "Is there any coffee?"

"I think there's still a pot on the fire."

McConnell stood up and took up his rifle.

"Get some sleep."

"I'm going to try," Pike said.

CHAPTER SIXTEEN

Pike went to his blanket and laid his rifle down next to it. Walking Star held the blanket open for him, and when he slid in next to her she brought the blanket down around both of them.

It became immediately evident that she considered this later.

Her mouth sought his and found it, and her hands fumbled with his pants. He wanted to protest, but even that might have been heard by the others. Although there was considerable room between him and the rest of the camp—because of Walking Star, he thought—he still wasn't sure that they would go unheard—unless they were very quiet.

She finally got his pants open and reached inside for him. She gasped as she took hold of him, tightening her hand and kissing his throat. He reached to the neck of her dress and inside for one breast. He cupped it, feeling the nipple harden in his palm.

She kissed, hungrily, and tried to work his pants down over his hips. He lifted his buttocks to help her, and when he was sufficiently exposed he reached down and slid her dress up her thighs until his hands encountered her bare butt.

She slid atop him beneath the blankets and he could feel the wiry hair between her legs, and the heat emanating from there. He took her by the hips and lifted her, and when she came down he was inside of her.

"Ooooh," she moaned against his neck, and they began to move together. As quiet as they were trying to be, the movement beneath the blanket would be unmistakable to anyone watching—only he hoped no one was watching.

Her breathing began to come faster and faster against his throat and he wasn't sure that she was going to be able to keep silent when the time came. Hell, for that matter he wasn't sure that *he* would be able to be quiet. It had been some time since he'd last lain with Angelique, and the explosion he felt building through his thighs and loins was not going to be a gentle one.

He cupped her muscular buttocks and pulled her close to him and finally released himself inside her. In her effort to keep silent she bit his shoulder, and it was all he could do not to cry out from *that*.

She relaxed on him then, her face nestled beneath his chin. He continued to rub her buttocks and when he had finally softened inside her she slid off him and lay on the blanket next to him.

"Thank you," she whispered, and in seconds she was asleep.

He pulled her dress down over her buttocks and thighs, and then lifted his hips so he could pull his trousers back up. He risked a peek over his shoulder at the camp, which seemed undisturbed, then took her in his arms and went to sleep.

*　　*　　*

He woke once during the night. Looking over his shoulder to see what had awakened him, he saw that McConnell was waking Kit Carson for his watch. They had all agreed that Stack should sleep through the night, since he was their main eyes and ears during the day.

He turned and saw Walking Star looking up at him with moist eyes.

"What is it?" he asked.

She smiled and said, "For the first time in many months, I am happy."

He leaned down and kissed her mouth gently, tasting her tears.

"Go to sleep," he whispered.

She nodded and closed her eyes.

The buffalo were still there the next morning, having only milled about somewhat, so without delay they started to shoot.

When the shooting started, the herd moved off a bit more slowly now, and they were able to bag more animals than they had before. Again, Walking Star had loaded faster than any of the others, and Pike had taken down the most buffalo.

While they busied themselves skinning the animals, Walking Star once again prepared a meal for them, since they had skipped any kind of breakfast in favor of an early start.

"Well, we're pretty well laden-down now," McConnell said.

"We have room for more," Carson said.

"Not if we're going to have to run from Comanche," McConnell said. "Maybe we should unload what we have, and then come back."

"We're here now," Carson said. "We should get as

much as we can, because we may not be able to come back here again."

They put it to a vote—with the three Delaware not consulted—decided to stay and either track the herd or find another.

They loaded up all the skins they had collected, and some meat, and continued on.

CHAPTER SEVENTEEN

"The woman is with them."

Strong Elk looked at Two-Faces, and found that he could not disagree.

She was not dead, because they had not found any trace of her body. Her trail had ended when it crossed the trail of shod ponies.

"That is more reason to catch up to them," Strong Elk said, "which we will do today."

Two-Faces now knew what Hawk Moon and He-Who-Takes-Many-Scalps already knew, that for some reason their leader, Strong Elk, was obsessed with this Crow woman.

Later that day they reached the second point where the whites had massacred their buffalo, and when they got there, found Black Bear and the rest of the braves. Their number had now swelled to more than sixty men and—in that final group—there were also twelve women.

"This is a crime against the Comanche which must be punished," Black Bear said.

"And it shall," Strong Elk said. "Come, we ride hard until we catch them—and then we make them pay."

PART THREE

MULE FORT

CHAPTER EIGHTEEN

Again they encountered a stretch of land that was all but barren. There was some brush and some stones, but nothing that would offer them any kind of effective cover, should the need arise.

That was the way both Pike and McConnell found themselves thinking. If the Comanche caught up to them at this point, they'd be hard-put to find some cover. Their only advantage over the Comanche would be that they were armed with rifles, while the Comanche would be armed only with bows and arrows. Still, a lack of cover would overcome any advantage they had—as would the superior number that the Comanche would certainly have.

Behind him Pike could feel Walking Star's body, as taut as a bow string. She was expecting the worst. Pike didn't know what Kit Carson was expecting. Carson was a legend among mountain men, certainly on a par with Jim Bridger, but if he had a fault, it was that he feared nothing. Pike felt that it was important for a man to have fears, and to know what they were. A man without fear often made wrong choices, even if they were for the right reasons.

Pike often experienced fear, and was on the verge

of feeling it now.

Joe Stack was riding up ahead of them, in plain sight because of the flatness of the land. To the far left were the mountains, but closer still there were some hills. Pike was looking that way and saw what he thought was a flock of blackbirds flying just above the hilltops. Soon enough he realized that he was mistaken.

What he saw were the heads of the Comanche as they crested the hill, riding toward the hunting party at full gallop. Pike couldn't see how many there were, but there were plenty.

At that moment he heard Joe Stack shout, "Injuns!"

The hilltop suddenly sprouted lances and feathers and the naked torsos of Indians, and then the hilltop was covered with Indians.

"Those are Comanche!" Joe Stack shouted.

"Must be a hundred of them!" McConnell shouted.

The Comanche were the best-mounted of any of the Indian tribes. They had the best horses, and the best riders, and this party was no different. The air was split by their blood-curdling war cries.

"Not a chance in hell of outrunning them!" McConnell said. Not even if they dumped their mules and skins and took off without them.

Pike looked at Kit Carson and said, "You know what that means, Kit!"

Carson nodded and shouted, "Mule fort!"

He grabbed for the reins of one of the mules, who was shying away, trying to run from the oncoming, screaming Comanche.

The mule tried to rear, but Carson held tight to the reins, and as the animal lifted his head, he brought his scalp knife across the throat, splitting it easily. Warm blood flowed over his arm and the animal fell over. He turned to look at the others, and saw that they were doing the same.

Pike, McConnell, and the others were leading the mules into a circle, and then slitting their throats so that when the carcasses fell, they formed a circle.

Right now a dead mule was worth a lot more than a live one.

Before the fallen animals could even stop kicking, Pike, McConnell, and Carson had thrown themselves down behind them and fired at the oncoming Comanche. While they reloaded, the three Delaware and Joe Stack fired, and they alternated, so that they were never reloading at the same time.

The Comanche, realizing that the whites had gotten themselves some cover, began to ride around them, firing their arrows in an arc in an attempt to get them over the mules.

They could feel the ground shaking from the horses' hooves. Pike could see the whites of the Comanches' eyes, and imagined that he could feel their very *breath* on him.

They continued to fire, first Pike, McConnell and Carson, then the three Delaware. Joe Stack held back and fired whenever it appeared there might be a lull. If there was even the shortest span of time without a shot, the Comanche might become bolder and charge them.

This went on for what seemed like hours, and finally the Comanche decided to draw back and take stock of the situation.

"Hold your fire!" Kit Carson shouted. "They're pulling back!"

They all took the time to make sure their weapons were loaded, and watched as the Comanche withdrew as far as the front slope of the hill, and dismounted.

"Anybody hit?" Pike asked.

Everyone answered negatively.

"They'll try again soon," Joe Stack said.

"Well, we got no place to go," Pike said. "Let's get ready."

On cue they all removed their knives and began to dig, trying to deepen their "fort," and increase their cover. Walking Star watched the Comanche, waiting for them to make their second charge. Pike was right next to her, digging as quickly as he could. Every so often he looked up to check the situation.

Pike looked around and saw that their horses had run off. If and when they made their getaway, it was going to have to be on foot.

The bodies of the mules were covered with arrows sticking out of them, and Pike wondered who was going to run out of ammo first, they or the Comanche.

From what he could see around them, there were four bodies lying on the ground. They must have hit more than that, but only four of them had fallen off their horses. The others were either wounded and had remained on their horses, or had died on their horses.

They were still digging, sweat pouring off their chins, grunting with the effort, when Walking Star called out,"They are coming again!"

"Let's go," Pike shouted.

They all grabbed their rifles and leaned on the mules, waiting for the Indians to get within range. Walking Star got behind Pike, so she could take his rifle and reload. They'd save their pistols in case the Comanche got much closer.

"All right, boys," Kit Carson yelled, "let's make every shot count."

CHAPTER NINETEEN

The Comanche changed their tactics.

When they made their initial charge this time they split in two, going by the mule fort on either side. When they reached the other side, they turned and made the same kind of charge again, splitting and going by on either side of them.

With each charge the Comanche were coming a bit closer and, as out of character as it was, the Delaware overreacted. They fired too soon after Pike, Carson and McConnell, and didn't have time to reload. Stack fired his rifle, but there was still a lull that the Comanche noticed.

The Comanche came closer and Pike pulled his Kentucky Pistol, in preparation for using it.

Suddenly, the Comanche stopped, and Pike saw the leader out front. It was apparent that he was Strong Elk, and further that he and Joe Stack had seen each other.

"Stack," Strong Elk shouted, "I see you. I will have your hair!"

"Come and get it, then," Stack called, and Pike tensed for the charge.

The Comanche let out their war cry and urged

their horses forward on the run. They launched their lances, which were tied to their belts for the purpose of recovery. The lances fell short, but the Indians kept coming.

Pike stood and aimed his Kentucky Pistol, as did Carson and McConnell, but suddenly the horses in front of the charge stopped and reared.

"What the—" McConnell said.

"It's the blood," Pike called out. "The horses don't like the smell of the mules' blood."

By this time the Delaware had reloaded, and Walking Star handed Pike his rifle.

"Fire!" Pike yelled.

The Indians were still fighting for control of their horses. Carson and McConnell fired their pistols, then hurriedly reloaded their rifles while Pike and the Delaware reloaded.

The Comanche, regaining control of their horses through superb horsemanship, withdrew, and then took their horses around the mule fort. They once again retreated to the base of the hill.

"That was close," Carson said.

"Well, let's not think on it," Pike said. "We still have some digging to do. Let's get to it."

Darkness fell and the Comanche hadn't launched another charge.

"What are they waiting for?" McConnell asked.

"What does it matter?" Pike asked. "As long as they're waiting they're not charging us."

"They're trying to come up with another strategy," Carson said. "Their horses don't like the blood, so maybe they'll charge us on foot, next time."

"Don't know that I'd mind that so much,"

McConnell said. "They'd make easier targets that way."

"You know," Pike said, "if they came straight at us and never veered, they'd overrun us for sure."

"Then why don't they?" McConnell asked.

"I just got a real uncomfortable thought," Kit Carson said.

"What's that?"

"What if they're waiting for more help?"

"You mean seven against sixty or seventy isn't good enough odds for them?"

"Strong Elk is a coward," Joe Stack said.

They all turned and looked at Stack.

"How did he get to be their leader?" Pike asked.

"He is a bully *and* a coward."

"Doesn't say much for the rest of his people."

"He is the son of a chief," Stack said. "That automatically gains him respect."

"Don't seem right," McConnell said.

"It ain't," Joe Stack said.

"Say, he knew who you were, Joe," McConnell said. Skins didn't know the story of Stack and Strong Elk.

"We know each other."

"I guess you weren't friends, huh?"

Stack didn't answer.

"I didn't think so."

"Think we can get some meat off one of them mules?" Pike asked.

The fallen mules had been piled high with skins, and a couple of them had their supplies.

"If they haven't fallen on it," Carson said.

He moved to one of the supply mules and had to pull out a good dozen arrows before freeing the sack with the meat in it.

93

"Well," he said, handing out hunks of meat, "at least we eat."

"Tomorrow, when the sun comes up," McConnell said, "we're gonna want to drink, too."

"Maybe that's what they're waiting for," Pike said.

"What?" McConnell said.

"For us to die of thirst."

CHAPTER TWENTY

"We are many; they are few," Two-Faces said.

"They cannot stand against us," He-Who-Takes-Many-Scalps said.

"They are too few," Black Bear said.

Strong Elk heard them all, but ignored them, as well. *He* was the leader, and *he* would make all the decisions.

Rushing them could cost many men. Strong Elk wanted the woman, but he knew that his people would rebel if he lost too many men trying to get her. And he would still have to explain it to his father.

"We must do something," Black Bear said. "We have already lost too many braves to them."

"We will do something," Strong Elk said.

"What, cousin?" Two-Faces asked.

"I will tell you when the time comes," Strong Elk said. "Now leave me. I must think."

The other three braves exchanged looks, and then moved away from Strong Elk. None of the three were strong enough to stand against him, and it did not dawn on them to stand against him, together.

Not yet, anyway.

*　　*　　*

Alone, Strong Elk thought about the Crow woman, Walking Star, but she was no longer the main reason he wanted to take the whites.

Now there was Joe Stack.

Strong Elk remembered the promise Joe Stack had made to him after Stack's wife was killed—and Strong Elk had killed her. Stack had never been able to make Strong Elk's people believe that Strong Elk had killed the daughter of the medicine man, but *Stack* believed it—he *knew* it, and had promised that he would kill Strong Elk before either of their lives had ended.

Now Joe Stack was back, and he was down there with the other whites. Stack had to be killed, now that he was here, within Strong Elk's reach.

Strong Elk knew what he was, and he wanted to keep anyone else from finding out. The way to do that was to kill Joe Stack. If he didn't, Stack would be back someday, and Strong Elk was tired of waiting.

CHAPTER TWENTY-ONE

When the sun came up they were all awake.

"Anybody get any sleep?" Pike asked.

"I dozed," McConnell said.

"So did I," Carson said.

Pike had drifted off from time to time, as well.

The Delaware, however, had all remained awake, as had Joe Stack. Walking Star had fallen asleep against Pike's shoulder.

They were all awake now, though, and watchful.

"Any meat left?" Pike asked.

They divvied up what was left, and that was the end of it. They had some dried beef left, but whatever coffee and bacon they had left was on the underside of one of the dead mules. It might as well have been a hundred miles away.

"What do you think they're doing?" McConnell asked, looking out toward where the Comanche were.

It was Joe Stack who answered.

"They're waiting for Strong Elk."

"To do what?" McConnell asked.

"To decide how bad he wants me," Joe Stack said.

McConnell gave Stack a puzzled look, then moved

it to Pike and Carson in turn.

When nobody volunteered to enlighten him he said, "Well, obviously there's something I don't know about, here."

He looked at them all again and finally Pike took it upon himself to clear it up somewhat.

"Let's just say that Strong Elk and Stack have an old score to settle," Pike said.

"A personal score?"

"Yes," Joe Stack said, still staring straight ahead, "very personal."

McConnell looked at Pike, and if he might have been tempted to pursue the matter further, a headshake from Pike warned him off.

"Well," he muttered to himself, "sometimes it *is* nice to know what you're dyin' for."

Walking Star shuffled over closer to Pike and asked, "There are other matters, now, than Strong Elk wanting me, Pike?"

"Yes, Walking Star," Pike said. "Other, much older matters."

"Then if we die it will not be my fault?"

"No," he said, "not your fault."

She smiled at him and said, "That makes my heart happier."

He touched her cheek and said, "At your age your heart should always be happy."

"It will be, as long as I am with you," she said, leaning into his hand. "Even if we die, I will be happy that we die together."

Pike had been thinking about that. He was trying to decide whether Walking Star would be better off with the Comanche, or better off dead. If he decided that she'd be better off dead, then he would save the ball in his Kentucky Pistol for her. If they were overrun he would make sure the Comanche did not take her alive.

It would be the last thing he did before his own death.

Which, he hoped, was not imminent.

The morning passed with no move from the Comanche.

The sun was high overhead now, beating down on them mercilessly, and they were all parched.

"Here," Joe Stack said. From his possibles sack he took a handful of small stones. "Put these in your mouths."

The small, round stones would aid them somewhat in creating saliva, but that was only a stop-gap measure. Soon they would begin to dehydrate.

"They don't have any water, either," McConnell said, "do they?"

"Comanche are used to going without water," Joe Stack said.

Pike looked at Stack. He didn't seem too much the worse for wear. He could probably go longer without water than any of them, except for the Delaware. It was Pike, Carson and McConnell who would feel the effects of the sun before anyone—including Walking Star.

"Will they make a charge today, Joe?" Pike asked. "They won't let a whole day go by without a try, will they?"

"No," Stack said. "At some point they'll want to test us. We'll have to be on our guard."

Walking Star looked at Pike, her eyes filled with sorrow for his suffering. Her lips touched his dried, cracked lips. He tried to grin, but it was painful, causing the skin on his lips to split.

"I see something," Stack said suddenly.

99

The others, who had been sitting with their backs against the dead mules, got up on their knees to have a look. The mule carcasses were starting to smell, and they were attracting hordes of flies.

"What is it?" Pike asked.

"Just some movement."

There was a small rise between them and the hill, so that they couldn't see the Comanche unless they were moving around—which they seemed to be doing now.

"They must be getting ready for a run," Kit Carson said.

"That's great," Pike said. "We can't do any more than we've been doing, but we're just holding them off. We're not hurting them."

"There's one way we can hurt them," Joe Stack said.

"Yeah," Carson said. "If we hit their leader, they may turn and run."

"Strong Elk," Pike said.

"When they split," Joe Stack said, "each half will have a leader."

"And if we hit one of them?"

"If it's not Strong Elk," Stack said, "we may just give them some pause, but if we get Strong Elk, they'll turn, run and regroup."

"Will they do that just because we hit one man?" McConnell asked, playing devil's advocate.

"Not only because we hit their leader," Stack said, "but because we're seven and we've been holding them off. Without Strong Elk, they'll be confused. They'll have to pull back, if just to choose a new leader."

"All right, then," Carson said. "When they go right and left those of us on the right go for the leader of that pack; those of us on this side do the same here.

One of them will be Strong Elk."

"The other will be Black Bear," Joe Stack said. "He's next in line to be medicine man."

"Medicine man?" Pike said.

"He is the medicine man's son."

Jesus, Pike thought, that makes him Stack's brother-in-law.

Quickly, Stack described the kind of war paint Black Bear and Strong Elk would be wearing. It was distinctive enough that they would stand out from the rest of the braves.

"They might hang back some so they can't be readily identified as the leaders," he suggested. "It will be important to recognize their paint."

"Everybody got it?" Carson asked.

They all said they did.

"There is one more," Stack said.

"Who?" Carson asked.

"Hawk Moon," Stack said. "He is Strong Elk's cousin. His paint will be similar to Strong Elk's."

"All right," Carson said, "we've got our targets. Don't anyone get careless. If you get careless, you get dead in a hurry."

"Listen," Stack said.

They fell silent and heard it. The sound of approaching horses. They all got up into position with their rifles, leaning over the dead mules, trying to ignore the smell and the flies.

"Here they come!" Stack shouted.

CHAPTER TWENTY-TWO

The Comanche came over the rise, their war cries splitting the air.

"Don't fire yet," Carson said, sighting along the barrel of his rifle.

Pike was looking down the barrel of his own rifle, trying to pick out the war paint that Joe Stack had described to him.

"Not yet," Carson shouted, as they got closer.

When they were almost on them Pike thought for a moment they weren't going to split, but were going to ride right over them.

"Now!" Carson shouted, and they fired.

Pike watched the half that split his way and recognized Black Bear from Stack's description. He sighted carefully, and as the braves went by he fired, and saw his ball strike Black Bear and drive him from his horse.

On the other side Joe Stack had Strong Elk in his sights, but he didn't want Strong Elk to die this way. To die on a battlefield was a death with honor. He wanted to dishonor Strong Elk before he killed him. He moved the barrel of his rifle, found his ex-brother-in-law, Hawk Moon, and fired.

His ball struck Hawk Moon squarely in the chest, and he saw another ball strike him high on the shoulder.

Kit Carson had Strong Elk in his sights, but as he fired he saw a ball strike the Comanche leader in the shoulder. That ball saved Strong Elk's life, for it spun the man around on his horse, causing Carson's ball to miss. For a moment, Strong Elk hung there precariously, almost off his horse, and then somehow righted himself.

Arrows arced toward them and thudded into the mule carcasses, and into the dirt around them. Pike was amazed that they so far had gone without any injuries.

The charge went by; they regrouped on the other side and came back. The white men and the Delaware fired again as they went by, and then the Comanche were gone, back to the base of the hill.

"Anybody hit?" Pike shouted.

"I am, damn it!" McConnell shouted.

Pike turned to his friend and saw an arrow sticking out of his thigh.

"Damned thing fell from the sky," McConnell said, through clenched teeth.

They looked around further and saw that they had also lost one of the Delaware. Jonesy was lying on his back with two arrows in his chest, his sightless eyes staring at the sky.

He had gotten careless.

"Sit still," Pike said. Joe Stack came over to examine McConnell's wound, and the others left it to him.

"The arc must have been high," he said, "and it struck without much force. It's not deep."

"That's good, ain't it?"

"That depends," Stack said. "If it was deep I could

103

break off the shaft and push it through. This way I might have to pull it out. That will bring some meat with it."

"Oh, great."

"Which way?" Carson asked.

Stack examined the wound again and then said, "I'd better pull it out. If I push it through I'll have to create another wound on the other side."

"Do what you have to do," McConnell said, "but stop talking and do it!"

While Stack worked over McConnell with the help of Walking Star, Pike and Carson and the remaining two Delaware watched for the Comanche.

"Somebody hit Strong Elk," Carson said to Pike, "and caused me to miss. He's wounded, but I couldn't tell how bad."

Not bad enough to die, Joe Stack hoped silently.

"I hit Black Bear," Pike said, "and saw him hit again. He's lying out there."

"So is Hawk Moon," Joe Stack said from behind them. "I killed him."

Pike was surprised for a moment, until he realized that Stack probably wanted to kill Strong Elk face-to-face.

They all reloaded and got up on their mules, waiting to see if the Comanche would come back.

By this time Stack had the arrow out of McConnell's leg and had bound the wound. He bound it tightly because he was unable to make a fire to cauterize the wound. The bleeding was going to have to stop by itself.

"How are you doing?" Pike asked McConnell.

"Fine," McConnell said, but Pike could see his friend was in pain. Luckily, he was retaining some of his color, indicating that he had not gone into shock.

104

As if to prove that he was all right, McConnell moved over to the dead Delaware and relieved him of anything they'd be able to use, including his rifle, powder horn and possibles sack.

"They're licking their wounds, now," Joe Stack said. "They'll find out that they lost Hawk Moon and Black Bear. Depending on how bad Strong Elk is hurt—well, I don't think they'll try again soon."

"You think they'll withdraw?" McConnell asked.

"They might," Joe Stack said, "but not all the way. They won't be able to believe that seven men held them off. They'll have to come back, just to prove to themselves that it can't be done."

"How will we know if they leave?"

"Oh, we'll see them leave," Stack said. "They'll make sure we see them. It'll be obvious—so obvious that we'll have to suspect a trap. Maybe we'll wait too long to leave and by then they'll be back."

"But we won't wait, will we?" McConnell asked.

"At the first sign that they've left," Carson said, "we'll have to start running."

"Stop asking so many questions," Pike said to his friend, "and get some rest."

"I'm fine."

"I know you are."

"I am!"

"Fine."

"Right."

Kit Carson stared at the two of them for a moment, wondering if that was a rehearsed exchange.

"How far to the nearest water, Joe?" Carson asked.

"About thirty miles."

That number hung in the air for them all to ponder.

"We can make that," Carson said.

"Hell," Stack said, "I've walked that far over a mountain. The plains should be easy."

Yeah, Pike thought, only in the mountains you didn't have to deal with that damned plains sun, and an arrow wound in the thigh.

Pike would get McConnell through, though, even if he had to carry him.

CHAPTER TWENTY-THREE

He-Who-Takes-Many-Scalps bent over Strong Elk and examined the wound.

"It is not very bad," he said. "The white man's ball went right through."

One of the braves had scraped up some mud and slapped it on the entry and exit wounds. The mud had been made by many of the braves urinating into the sand.

"Where is Black Bear?" Strong Elk asked.

"He is dead," He-Who-Takes-Many-Scalps answered. "So, too, is Hawk Moon."

"We have lost much," Strong Elk said.

"And almost more," He-Who-Takes-Many-Scalps said. "We must withdraw."

Strong Elk's first instinct was to say no, but he knew that what He-Who-Takes-Many-Scalps said was true. They would have to withdraw, and regroup, and tend to his wound properly. The women—who had been left just on the other side of the hill—would have to mourn the loss of Black Bear, the son of a medicine man, and Hawk Moon, Strong Elk's cousin.

"All right," Strong Elk said. "Get me on my pony

and we will withdraw."

"When they see us go they will come out and attempt to escape," He-Who-Takes-Many-Scalps said.

"They will be on foot," Strong Elk said. "The next time we catch them they will have no mules to hide behind."

He-Who-Takes-Many-Scalps and another brave lifted Strong Elk to his feet and helped their leader mount his horse.

Strong Elk waited for the other braves to mount up, seething inside. He knew that it was not Joe Stack's ball that had wounded him. Stack would want to kill him face-to-face. Still, there would be some small satisfaction in Stack that he and his comrades had driven the Comanche off.

"We are ready," He-Who-Takes-Many-Scalps said, riding up next to his leader.

"We go," Strong Elk said.

They started up the hill, and when they reached the top Strong Elk stopped and looked back. He couldn't actually see Joe Stack, but he knew that he and Stack were looking at each other.

Enjoy your satisfaction, he thought, for the short time you will have it, Stack.

I will find you, and I will have you.

CHAPTER TWENTY-FOUR

When it got dark Joe Stack said, "Wait here and I will go check."

No one argued. One man could move more silently than two.

Stack eased over one of the mules, pushing the arrows out of the way. The mules were so covered with arrows that you could not put your hand down anywhere without touching a shaft.

"Let's collect what we're going to bring," Carson said to the others.

"There isn't much," Pike said. "Whatever blankets we can pull off the mules, our knives and guns. Anything else would just weigh us down."

Carson looked longingly at all the skins they had collected.

"It would have been a glorious hunt."

"We knew we were coming to Comanche country," Pike said. "We knew that would mean Comanche."

"What we didn't know was that Joe Stack had a private beef with them," McConnell pointed out.

"I knew," Carson said. "He's my friend."

Pike and McConnell looked at Carson, and then McConnell said, "I'm sorry. I shouldn't have said that."

"No, you're right," Carson said. "When I invited you along I should have told you the whole story. I knew Joe would be hoping to catch up to Strong Elk."

"Yeah, but we didn't know Strong Elk would catch up to us," McConnell said.

And, of course, they were all thinking of Walking Star. Picking her up had certainly put the Comanche on their trail, initially.

"Next time we go hunting," Pike said, "I suggest we just hunt."

"Amen," McConnell said.

They went to work, pulling blankets off the mules, getting their weapons together. Walking Star offered to carry something and they gave her the dead Delaware's knife and rifle.

That done, they settled down to wait for Stack to return.

An hour later Pike said, "He should have been back by now."

"He'll be back," Carson said.

"What if something's gone wrong?" McConnell asked. "What if the Comanche didn't leave, and they were waiting for him?"

"We'd know," Carson said.

"How?" McConnell asked.

"If they had him they wouldn't kill him quietly," Carson explained. "They'd make sure that we heard every scream."

"So then we just wait," McConnell said.

"We just wait," Carson said.

Another half hour passed and suddenly Carson said, "Here he comes."

Joe Stack appeared and climbed back over the dead mules.

"We were wondering what happened," McConnell said.

"I wanted to make sure they weren't nearby, waiting for us to leave so they could ride us down."

"And?"

"It's all clear," Stack said. "They pulled back completely."

"For how long?" Carson asked.

"No way of telling," Stack said. "We're going to have to get moving as soon as possible."

"We're ready to go," Carson said.

Stack picked up his rifle and a blanket and said, "So let's go."

They stood up and climbed over the mule carcasses. Pike helped Walking Star over, pushing some of the arrows out of her way.

"How are you doing?" Pike asked McConnell.

"I'll be fine," McConnell said, but Pike could already see that he was limping badly.

"We'll walk a while before we start to trot," Stack said.

"I'm fine!" McConnell said again.

"It's not for your benefit," Stack said. "We should just start out slowly.

Stack took the lead and they started walking north, toward the closest water, thirty miles away.

Pike saw something hanging from Joe Stack's belt, and then he knew what had taken him so long. There were two scalps dangling from his left side.

Undoubtedly, one of them belonged to his ex-brother-in-law, Black Bear. Pike was willing to bet that the other one came from the head of Hawk Moon, Black Elk's cousin.

Joe Stack had left a little message behind.

111

CHAPTER TWENTY-FIVE

They walked for the first mile or two. Contrary to what he had said, Stack was trying to make it easier for McConnell to keep up. Eventually, though, he was forced to go into a steady dogtrot if they were going to have a chance of putting some distance between them and the Comanche.

Stack had the lead, followed by the two Delaware Indians, Kit Carson, Pike and Walking Star and finally, Skins McConnell.

More and more as they went on, McConnell began to lag back, limping badly. Finally, Pike had to turn back and see to his friend, and Walking Star went with him.

"Skins—"

"I'm all right," McConnell said, stopping and sitting down a moment. "I just have to rest a moment."

Pike leaned over to examine the wound and saw that it was bleeding profusely. Pretty soon McConnell would have lost too much blood to continue.

"We've got to stop this bleeding," Pike said. "I'll have to make a fire."

"No," McConnell gasped, "that'll take too long."

"Walking Star, run up ahead and tell Carson and

Stack what we're doing here. Tell them to keep on going and we'll catch up."

"Yes, I will," she said. "I will return—"

"No," Pike said, "you go on with them. Skins and I will catch up."

"No," she said, "I will continue."

Before he could argue she was gone, moving very quickly.

"Sit still," Pike said. "I'm going to gather some makings for a fire."

"All right," McConnell said, beyond arguing.

When Pike returned with some brush and twigs, McConnell was lying on his back. The land around them was so barren Pike had barely been able to gather enough makings for a fire.

He was trying to scrape what he had together in a pile when Walking Star reappeared, followed by Kit Carson. They had both picked up whatever they could on the way back to use in making a fire, and they added it to what Pike had gathered.

"What are you doing here?" Pike asked Carson.

"Came back to help. Stack and the Delaware are scouting out ahead."

"It's not ahead we have to worry about," Pike said. "It's behind."

Once they had the fire going, Pike rested his knife in the flame, waiting for it to heat sufficiently.

While he did that, Carson went to the prone McConnell and cleared the wound.

"How you doing, Skins?"

"Just great, Kit," McConnell said, weakly. "I'll be on my feet in a few minutes."

"Sure you will."

A few moments later, McConnell was unconscious. Walking Star covered him with a blanket and then lifted his head into her lap.

"He's out," Carson told Pike as Pike leaned over McConnell with his knife.

"It's just as well," Pike said. "This is gonna hurt like the dickens."

Carson held McConnell's arms down in case the man came awake while Pike was cauterizing the wound.

"Here we go," Pike said, and touched the hot steel to the bleeding wound. They all smelled scorched flesh, and then Pike removed the knife to examine the wound.

"All right, let's bind it," Pike said.

"I will bind it," Walking Star said. She lifted McConnell's head gently and put a second blanket beneath it, then took Pike's shirt and tore strips from it to bind the wound.

Pike and Carson took the time to sit and get some rest, themselves.

"I don't think we'll catch up to Stack and the Delaware," Carson said.

"Maybe it's better this way," Pike said. "We split into two groups, and maybe at least one group will get through and get to safety."

"Maybe."

"In fact," Pike said, "why don't you take Walking Star and start moving? You and she can make better time alone while I help McConnell."

Kit Carson saw the wisdom in that, but asked, "Do you think she'll go with me?"

"I'll talk to her," Pike said. "She'll go. There's no point in anyone else getting slowed down by Skins's wound. I'm his friend; I'll take care of him."

"Well, if you can convince her, I'm game," Carson said. "Maybe split in three we can all slip through the Comanches' fingers."

Walking Star came over at that moment and said,

"His wound is bound and the bleeding has stopped, but he needs water."

"We'll get to water soon enough," Pike said. "Sit down, Walking Star. We have to talk."

Carson got up and went to McConnell's side, leaving Pike and Walking Star alone.

"What is it?"

"I want you to go with Kit Carson."

"No—"

"Don't tell me no," Pike said, cutting her off. "I want us all to get through this, and the way we do that is to split up. McConnell is my friend and he will be my responsibility. I won't be able to look out for you, but Kit will. I can trust him to take care of you."

She stared at him for a few moments, then said, "I want to stay with you, but I will do as you ask."

"I knew I could count on you," Pike said. "Come, let's get you started."

He stood up and helped her to her feet and they walked over to where Carson sat next to the prone McConnell.

"He's still unconscious."

"He'll be stronger when he wakes up," Pike said. "Why don't you and Walking Star get moving? You can cover a lot of ground before daybreak."

Pike handed Walking Star over to Carson, who took her hand.

"Keep heading north," Carson said, "and we'll meet again soon."

"On the other side of the Cimarron," Pike said.

He could tell by the look on Carson's face that Kit had his doubts about Pike being able to get across the Cimarron with the wounded McConnell. Well, Pike would drag him or carry him if he had to, but he'd get him across, because if the tables were turned McConnell would do the very same for him.

Pike and Carson shook hands, and then Pike touched Walking Star's face.

"Trust Kit and do what he says."

"I will."

Carson started trotting then, pulling Walking Star behind him. She looked back over her shoulder as long as she could, and then finally had to turn to keep up with Kit Carson.

Pike leaned over McConnell and saw that his friend was breathing deeply and evenly. He checked the wound and there wasn't even a trickle of blood. Walking Star had bound it well.

The fire he had built for the knife had gone out, and he spread the ashes now. He had no further makings for a fire, so they would have to do without. Pike made sure McConnell was well covered and then sat down next to his friend and stared longingly at the two blankets, one covering his friend and one under his head. Pike had no blanket and no shirt and finally lifted his friend's head into his lap and wrapped *that* blanket around himself.

He took his Kentucky Pistol out of his belt, held it down by his side, and kept watch over his fallen friend for the rest of the night.

CHAPTER TWENTY-SIX

Pike felt McConnell stir and looked down at his friend's face. McConnell's eyes fluttered open and then squinted against the daylight.

"Good morning," Pike said.

"Morning?" McConnell said. "Jesus, what—let me up."

"I'm not holding you down."

McConnell struggled to a seated position and looked around.

"Where is everyone?"

"They went on ahead to the water hole," Pike said. "From there they'll cross the Cimarron and meet us on the other side."

"And you stayed here with me," McConnell said. "You should have left me behind, Jack."

Pike fixed his friend with a glare and said, "Would you have left me behind?"

McConnell hesitated a moment, then said, "No."

"Then let's not discuss it. How's the leg?"

McConnell, surprised, looked down at his leg. Carefully, he flexed the knee and touched his thigh.

"It doesn't feel too bad."

"We got the bleeding stopped, but bound it pretty

tight. The only thing we don't have is some nourishment for you to replace the blood you lost."

"Just help me to my feet," McConnell said, "and we can get on our way."

Pike stood up and assisted McConnell to a standing position. McConnell was somewhat rocky, but remained on his feet.

"Dizzy?" Pike asked

"A bit."

"That's from loss of blood. If we only had some food for you."

"Forget it," McConnell said. "Let's get moving."

"Slowly, at first," Pike said, "until we see if your leg is going to hold up."

"All right."

They started walking, Pike staying close to his friend in case he suddenly keeled over.

Pike was thirsty, so he knew his friend had to be parched. How many miles had Stack said it was to the water hole?

Don't think about it, he told himself, just keep moving.

He was carrying both blankets, his rifle and his Kentucky Pistol. McConnell had his own rifle and pistol, and after a while even they would become extra heavy.

"Come on," McConnell said. "Let's pick it up."

"You lead," Pike said. "We'll move at your pace."

"Oh yeah?" McConnell said. "Well, see if you can keep up with me!"

McConnell started trotting ahead and Pike fell in behind him. The night's rest had done his friend a lot of good, but some food and water would serve him even better. If they even came across a rabbit, Pike was going to try to catch it.

But there were no rabbits; there were only the

barren plains, and they kept on running. Pike was surprised and impressed by his friend's resilience—and pleased.

Maybe they'd make it after all.

Stack and the Delaware reached the water hole and fell to their knees in front of it. Stack was taking water in both his hands and rubbing it over his dry face when he heard one of the Delaware grunt, followed by a splash. He looked up and saw the man lying on his face in the water, a Comanche arrow sticking out of his back.

"Move!" he shouted to the other Delaware, but his warning was too late. An arrow pierced the man's neck and he fell over, dead.

Stack stood then and looked around, his rifle held in both hands, but there was nothing to shoot at.

The water hole was surrounded by boulders and rock formations, and there could have been a Comanche behind every one of them.

And there probably was.

Kit Carson was impressed with Walking Star. Not only was she able to keep up with him, but he wouldn't have been surprised if she had left him behind.

"There it is," he said, pointing to the rock formations. "Joe said that the water hole was hidden by rocks."

"Water," she said, and it was the first hint she had given that she was thirsty.

They increased their pace and got to the water. Walking Star leaned over the water, reaching for it with her hands when she saw the first body. Carson heard her sharp intake of breath and came to her side.

"It's one of the Delaware," he said. He reached for the man's feet and pulled him from the water. "The other one must be farther in, submerged." He had no way of knowing how deep the water was.

He leaned over the Delaware and saw the wound. It had been made by an arrow, which had been removed.

"Comanche," he said.

He heard Walking Star's scream too late, and then the flash of pain as an arrow bit hard and deep.

It was almost dark when Pike and McConnell reached the water hole.

"There it is," Pike said.

"I . . . told you . . . we'd make it," McConnell said, between deep breaths.

"Come on, Skins," Pike said. "Let's get you some of that water."

They moved down among the rocks and immediately saw the bodies.

"Oh God," Pike said. He rushed ahead of McConnell and leaned over Kit Carson. There was an arrow sticking out of Carson's shoulder, and it was in deep, but he was still alive.

McConnell checked the Delaware and said, "He's dead." He stood up and stared at the water hole with his hands on his hips. "From the looks of it he was in there. The other one probably still is."

"Kit's alive," Pike said. "We've got to get this arrow out."

"Yeah, I know," McConnell said. "I'll tear my shirt into strips for bandages—and we'll need a fire."

"Start looking around for the makings," Pike said, tearing Carson's shirt around the wound. "Whatever

120

you can find."

"Right," McConnell said. "Pike?"

"Yeah?"

"What about Walking Star?"

Still bent over Carson, Pike said, "I'm trying not to think of that."

PART FOUR

COMANCHE HUNT

CHAPTER TWENTY-SEVEN

Pike bandaged Carson's wound as tightly as he could, after cauterizing it. In the immediate area of the water hole they were able to find some bushes from which to build a fire.

It was McConnell's turn to hold Carson down while Pike pressed the hot knife to the wound. When he smelled the flesh burning McConnell wrinkled his nose.

"Are you sure you did this to me?"

"You were unconscious, just as Kit is now," Pike reminded him.

Afterward they spread a blanket on the ground for Kit to lie on, and folded one to go beneath his head.

"This hunting trip has turned into a massacre," McConnell said.

"Sorry I talked you into it, Skins."

"You didn't talk me into it, Pike," McConnell said. "When have you ever talked me into doing something I didn't really want to do?"

"You're right," Pike said. "It's usually *you* who talks me into doing something I don't want to do."

"Like what?"

"Like fighting Big Bubba."

"Oh, yeah, that."

Pike sat down on the ground next to McConnell, who had his leg stretched out in front of him.

"How are you feeling?"

"Better," McConnell said. "The water helped. Of course, the heat doesn't help. We better keep giving Kit water. It'll keep his strength up."

"Yeah."

Every so often Pike would soak another piece of McConnell's shirt in water and squeeze it into Carson's mouth. He'd then use the cloth to wet Carson's face.

"How long are we going to have to stay here?" McConnell asked.

"You and Kit will stay until you're ready to travel," Pike said.

"And you?"

"I'm going after Walking Star and Joe Stack."

"You're going to trail the Comanche?"

"I have to."

"What if they're already dead?"

Briefly, Pike explained the relationship between Joe Stack and Strong Elk.

"Those two want to kill each other slowly," Pike finished. "If that wasn't the case, Stack's body would be lying here with the Delaware."

"You have a point," McConnell said, "but what can you do alone, and on foot?"

"I don't know," Pike said, "but I've got to try. I don't think you and Kit are quite ready to cross the Cimarron on foot. Maybe I can at least come up with some horses."

"Well," McConnell said, "when you put it that way, it makes sense."

Pike stood up and said, "I'm going to see if I can find some kind of game."

126

"What do you think you'll find around here?"

"Something that's attracted to water."

"And what about the Comanche?"

"I think they're gone from here. Strong Elk has what he wanted. In fact, I think they might even have thought they took care of everyone."

"Which would leave us in the clear."

"If that's what we want."

"And it's not?"

"No," Pike said, "it's not."

"That's what I thought."

"Keep an eye on Kit."

"Sure," McConnell said. "It's the least I can do."

Pike went to the water and splashed some on his sunburned torso. He was trying not to think about how much his skin hurt.

"Keep yourself wet," he suggested to McConnell, "unless you want to burn like me."

"Maybe we could both pass as Comanche," McConnell said.

"Not unless we found something to shave with," Pike said. "You don't see many Indians with a face full of whiskers."

"Good point."

Pike picked up his rifle and left.

"When you left here with your rifle, this isn't what I expected you to come back with," McConnell said.

Pike took another bite of rattlesnake and said, "Never mind. At least we don't have to eat it raw. Hey, make sure you save some for Kit."

"I'm saving *most* of it for Kit."

"Don't save most of it. You need the nourishment, too. I'll save most of this—"

At that moment Carson moaned. Pike leaned over

him and saw him open his eyes.

"Kit?"

The eyes fluttered and for a moment Pike thought they'd close again, but they stayed open.

"Pike?"

"Do you think you can sit up?"

Carson thought a moment, then said, "I'm willing to try."

Pike helped Carson to a seated position, leaning his back against a rock.

"Here," McConnell said. "Try eating something."

Carson took the piece of rattlesnake and bit into it. The juice dripped down over his chin.

"What happened?" he asked. "Where are the others?"

"The Delaware are dead," Pike said. "Stack and Walking Star are . . . gone. We assume they've been taken by Strong Elk."

"Pike, I'm sorry—"

Pike waved off his apology.

"It's not your fault, Kit," he said. "You couldn't have known the Comanche would be waiting here, and that arrow did hit you in the back."

"Aw, I should have been more careful."

"Don't berate yourself, Kit," Pike said. "There's nothing you can do about it now."

"But there's something *you* can do, right?" McConnell said.

"What do you mean?" Carson asked. He looked at Pike and said, "What are you going to do?"

"I'm going to get Stack and Walking Star away from Strong Elk."

"How the hell do you intend to do that?" Carson asked.

"I don't know," Pike said. "I'll figure something out."

"You can't do anything alone," Carson said, "and on foot—"

"I've already gone through this with him, Kit," McConnell said. "He's determined."

"I don't care how determined he is, Skins," Carson said. "He can't catch up to them on foot."

"Well, he's going to try," McConnell said, "and there's nothing either one of us can do to stop him."

Kit Carson was about to speak when they heard the sound of an approaching horse.

"Now who can that be?" McConnell said.

"I'll see," Pike said, taking up his rifle.

Pike moved over behind some rocks and stared out into the darkness. While talking with Carson and McConnell, he'd been sitting before the fire, so his night vision was not what it could have been.

"Hey!" he shouted, leaping aside.

It was a riderless horse, and it headed straight for the water hole and began to drink contentedly.

"It's one of our horses," McConnell said.

"It must have headed straight for the nearest water once it was able to smell it," Pike said.

"I wonder if the others will make it, also," McConnell said.

"They could have gone in a totally different direction from this one when they first scattered," Pike said. "I guess only time will tell."

He moved to the animal and saw that it was the horse Joe Stack had been riding, an able-bodied Indian pony. He checked the animal out while it was drinking and found that it was still able-bodied. It was still saddled, and all the supplies that it had been carrying were intact.

Pike dug into the saddlebags and came out with some dried beef and a small bag of coffee.

"Well, you guys can eat the dried beef," he said. "I

129

guess the coffee won't do us much good, since we don't have a pot."

He handed the meat to McConnell and Carson and continued to go through the saddlebags. There was nothing else that would be of much help.

"Well," he said, facing McConnell and Carson, "I guess this solves the problem of my being on foot."

"Well, then," Carson said, "the only thing you have to do now is find some way to singlehandedly take on the entire Comanche nation."

CHAPTER TWENTY-EIGHT

Joe Stack opened his eyes and sat up. Sitting up hurt, but he made it. He was sore all over, but especially in his ribs. He looked around the teepee and saw Walking Star sitting opposite him.

"I thought you were dead," she said, hugging her knees to her chest.

"No," he said, "not yet. Strong Elk would be smart to kill me right away, but he will not."

"Why?"

"Because he wants to make me suffer," Stack said, "just as I want to make him suffer."

"Then he will win."

"He has the upper hand now," Stack said, "but we will have to wait and see what the future brings."

At that moment a Comanche entered the teepee, threw a look at Stack, and then reached for Walking Star. She shrank back from him, but he grabbed her arm anyway.

"Go with him," Stack told her. "They won't hurt you."

"What about you?"

"Don't worry about me," Stack said. "Look after yourself. Remember, the others are still out there."

She nodded, stood up and went with the Comanche.

Joe Stack didn't even believe what he was telling her. If the Comanche had waited at the water hole long enough, then the others—Kit Carson, Jack Pike, Skins McConnell—were all dead. Walking Star was alive because Strong Elk wanted her.

Joe Stack was alive because Strong Elk wanted him.

In a totally different way.

The Comanche took Walking Star to another teepee, where Strong Elk was waiting for her.

"Leave us," Strong Elk told him.

Walking Star stood just inside the entrance, staring at Strong Elk.

"So," Strong Elk said, in English, "you survived."

She didn't speak.

"Come closer."

She took a step closer.

"Closer," he said.

She took another step. Strong Elk lost his patience. He stood up, crossed the teepee to her, and slapped her across the face.

"When I tell you to do something, you will obey!"

She put her hand to her cheek and said, "I will not."

"You will!"

"No."

He slapped her other cheek, rocking her head back. While she was off balance he took hold of her dress and tore it off her. Her bare breasts bobbed into view and she glared at Strong Elk, making no move to cover her nakedness.

"I have waited long enough for you, woman," he

132

said. "I will have you."

"You will have my body," she said to him, "but you will never have me."

He took hold of one of her breasts and twisted it cruelly. She whimpered and the pain took her to her knees. Strong Elk removed the loincloth he was wearing, exposing himself.

"I will have you in *every* way," he said. "Satisfy me, and you live."

Walking Star glared up at him, ignoring his exposed penis. She knew that the only chance she had to see Pike was to live.

"If you do not," Strong Elk went on, "you will die."

Slowly, reluctantly, she lowered her eyes.

CHAPTER TWENTY-NINE

Pike was sorry to have to saddle the horse again the next morning. The animal had been running around saddled for so long, the few hours it had had without the saddle hardly seemed enough.

"Here," McConnell said, handing Pike something wrapped in cloth.

"What's this? Not the rest of the jerky."

"No," McConnell said, with a small smile. "The rest of the snake."

Pike laughed and said, "Thanks."

"It's too bad you have nothing to carry water in," McConnell said.

"I'll find water," Pike said.

"How?"

"I've got a water finder right here," he said, patting the horse's neck. "We'll get along."

Kit Carson came over and handed Pike something tattered.

"What's this?"

"It's what's left of my shirt," Carson said. "You'll need it out there."

"You'll need it here," Pike said. "Besides, I can't get much more burned than this."

"After what I went through to get it off, just take it," Carson said.

"All right," Pike said. He leaned over and soaked the shirt in the water—as much to get the blood off as anything else—and then put it on. The water felt good on his burned skin.

"Maybe you won't blister so soon, this way," Carson said.

"Blisters are the least of my worries," Pike said.

"Jack," McConnell said.

"What?"

"Do you really think you have a chance to find them?" his friend asked.

"Skins, I've got to try. You know that."

"I know, I know."

"Wait for me here," Pike said.

"How long?"

"Until you get tired of waiting," Pike said, "or until you both feel strong enough to travel. Whichever comes first, I guess."

Pike saddled up and then accepted his rifle from McConnell. His Kentucky Pistol was tucked into his belt.

"Good luck," McConnell said, and Carson nodded his agreement.

"To the two of you, also."

He reined the horse around, started off, then stopped and turned in the saddle.

"Any of those other horses show up," he called out, "you use it to get out of here, you hear?"

"We hear," McConnell answered.

As Pike rode off, McConnell said to Carson, "What are we gonna do if one of the other horses does show up?"

"We're gonna go after him and help him," Kit Carson said. "What else?"

"Thank you," McConnell said.

Pike was more used to tracking things through the snow in the mountains than on the plains, but, riding with Joe Stack, he'd had no recourse but to learn something. Besides, how hard could it be to track fifty or sixty Comanche?

By noon, the first things he found were not Comanche, however, but a small herd of buffalo. He looked down at them longingly. Some cooked buffalo meat would go very nicely now, but he didn't want to take a chance on firing a shot, or on building a fire. He took out a piece of rattlesnake and popped it into his mouth.

He lamented not having something to carry water in, not so much for himself as for the horse. He hoped that the animal had drunk its fill. He knew that *he* had, but he was beginning to feel the effects of the sun.

He didn't push the animal, since it had traveled a long way during the past week. The trail he was following was fairly clear, but then the Comanche had no reason to think they were being tracked. At times the ground was too hard to betray any sign, so he'd just keep going in the same direction and eventually he'd see something. Scuff marks, chipped stones, droppings—both man and horse—told him that he was still on the right track.

If he lost the trail at any time and didn't pick it up again, he would backtrack until he saw something, and then start again.

When darkness began to fall, he camped and went to sleep early, so as to give himself and the horse some extra rest. Early the next morning he breakfasted on the last of the rattlesnake, and then started off again.

A lot was going to depend on luck; he knew that, but he'd always been pretty lucky. Evidence the fight with Big Bubba, and the fact that, after all they'd been through, with the Delaware dead, McConnell and Kit Carson wounded and Stack and Walking Star captured, he was still unhurt and free.

That was nothing if not pure luck.

CHAPTER THIRTY

Quite by accident, Pike stumbled onto the Comanche encampment.

He was studying the ground intently, looking for sign, when suddenly he heard horses ahead. He reined his horse in, and when he looked up, he saw the spires of the Comanche teepees. In fact, he saw several Comanche, and if they had looked up at that moment they would have seen him.

Keeping his head, he gently eased his horse backward and, when he felt it was safe, he turned the horse and rode a way away from the camp. When he turned and looked back he realized he could not see the camp from even a short distance. Although the ground seemed level, it actually had a curve to it. He was far enough away from the camp so that they couldn't see him and he couldn't see them.

He dismounted and grounded the reins of his horse. The animal would stay unless spooked, but there was nothing there to tie him to, so this would have to do.

He took his rifle, checked his Kentucky Pistol, and moved forward again on foot. After he'd walked about a hundred yards he got down on his hands and knees. The ground was hot on his hands, but he was able to stand it. After a while he was able to see the camp again, and he settled himself down onto his belly.

Darkness was about an hour away. He'd just have to stay there and wait.

While he waited, he wondered if someone would find his horse. Maybe he should have let the animal loose, but he had a horse now. Would it be wise to let it go now because he *might* be able to get one from the Comanche?

He decided to leave the horse where it was. Letting it loose didn't mean he wouldn't be discovered. Hell, they could have come riding in or out of camp and right over him at any moment. Once again he was relying on luck—and sooner or later that would rise up and bite him on the ass.

You could only push your luck so far—and he had the feeling his had been pushed to the brink.

It was dark.

There were some fires in the Comanche camp, but in general, activities had died down. If he knew what teepee Walking Star and Joe Stack were in, he could have sneaked down and tried to free them. The way it stood, he was going to need too much time. First he had to locate them, and then try to free them. He was going to have to wait until there was absolutely no activity in the camp, and that meant waiting until the middle of the night.

The Comanche must have felt they were camped in a safe place, because he couldn't see where they had set up any kind of a watch—and if there was a watch that he couldn't see, he would have been taken by now.

From what he knew about Strong Elk, the man lacked the real qualities of a leader. He was a bully and a coward, according to Stack, and here he had not set up a watch, so he was also overconfident.

All of that could work in Pike's favor.

The day's ride in the baking sun had drained him, and it was all he could do not to fall asleep lying there on the ground. At least, with the advent of night, the ground had cooled somewhat, but although he had been baking during the day, there was now the danger of being chilled.

Coming down to the plains had been an adventure, but he was sure it was not something he would want to do again. When he got back to his beloved mountains, he was going to stay there.

What he wouldn't have given for the sight of a little friendly snow.

There was still a fire in the camp, but now the activity had died down totally. In all the time he had been there he'd been given no inkling of where Walking Star or Stack might be held. He was going to have to go down and start looking, and hope that he was quiet enough not to wake Comanche.

He started by circling the camp. Judging by the number of horses that were picketed outside the camp, he decided that he was dealing with about sixty or seventy Comanche. There was no way of telling how many of those would be women, children or old people. He had to assume at this point that they were all braves.

Better to overestimate the enemy than under-estimate them.

He continued to circle the camp until he was back where he started. It was time to stop fooling around and go on into camp and find Walking Star and Joe Stack.

If they were even there at all.

CHAPTER THIRTY-ONE

Walking Star was sore.

Strong Elk had brutalized her repeatedly, raping her so violently that at one point he had started his wound bleeding.

He had left her in the teepee where he'd had her, telling her that it was now hers. He also warned her not to try to escape, because there was nowhere to go. After that he left to have his wound tended to, and had not returned.

She had fallen asleep then, and when she awoke she saw that it was dark outside. She crawled to the entrance of the tent and saw that there was a brave seated just outside to keep her from escaping.

She went back to the blanket and lay down, wondering if Pike would come for her. Why should he? What did she mean to him? She was just a squaw he had picked up on the trail.

He would come for Joe Stack, though. He was, after all, a white man, and friends with Kit Carson and Pike. Surely they would come for Stack—and maybe she could get them to take her with them.

Or perhaps she was being unfair to Pike. He had been so kind to her right from the beginning. It was possible that he did have feelings for her, just as she had very strong feelings for him. No white man had ever treated her so tenderly, before.

If she had to stay here with Strong Elk, she would kill herself.

It had been a rough day for Joe Stack.

Obviously, Strong Elk had told some of the braves that they could take the white man out and have some sport with him, so they had done just that.

First he had been forced to wrestle brave after brave until finally he was too exhausted and one of them finally defeated him. While he was lying on the ground trying to get his breath back they had all come over and taken turns kicking him. It was only the fact that they were mostly barefoot that kept him from being seriously injured. If they had been white men and wearing boots, his ribs would have been caved in, for sure.

After that they had treated him as if he were a dog— literally. They tied a leather thong around his neck and led him around camp on it, making him walk on all fours. Under normal circumstances he would not have submitted to such an indignity, but the truth was, he was too tired to fight it.

Soon the braves tired of playing with him, and one of them "walked" the dog back to his teepee and let him go inside. They had not even removed the leather "leash" from his neck.

He was so exhausted that he fell asleep with his leash still on.

When Stack woke up he could see that it was dark. He moved to the entrance of the teepee and saw that a brave had been positioned outside. He looked around inside the teepee for something to use as a weapon, but there was nothing. The teepee had been cleaned out before he had been put inside, just for that purpose.

He touched his neck where the leather leash had rubbed his skin raw, and began to remove it, when he realized that he did have a weapon.

It was around his neck.

Similarly, Walking Star was searching her teepee for a weapon, but there was nothing. Even if there had been, how could she have hoped to overpower the brave who was sitting outside?

She lay down again and prayed for Pike to come.

Stack had decided to wait until it was very late, until all activity in camp had died down, and then he would effect his escape. There was only one point on which he was undecided.

Once he was out of his teepee, should he escape, or try to find Walking Star and take her with him? She meant nothing to him, really, but she did mean something to Pike. There was also the prospect of leaving her behind, knowing what Strong Elk would do to her.

His decision was really very simple.

He would not leave Strong Elk another woman to kill.

In fact, he would not leave Strong Elk alive.

As Pike moved down closer to the camp, he saw that his luck was still running with him. There were two teepees that had braves seated in front of them. Apparently, Walking Star and Joe Stack had been separated, and both of them were under guard.

Well, Strong Elk had finally done something right, and it was going to work against him.

Pike thanked him.

Pike chose one of the teepees and began to work his way around behind it. He intended to cut through the fabric with his knife, effectively creating a back door. When that was done and he had freed whoever was inside, they would go to the other teepee and do the same thing.

He hadn't planned on help from inside.

Joe Stack wrapped some of the leather thong around each hand, and moved to the entrance of the teepee. As he poked his arms outside, the brave sat up straight, but as he turned to see what was happening, Stack brought the thong down over his head and wrapped it around his throat. The brave opened his mouth to shout, but nothing came out. Stack increased the pressure and dragged the brave into the tent at the same time. Inside, he pressed his knee to the small of the brave's back to increase his leverage, and crossed his hands so that the thong was wrapped round the man's throat.

As the brave fell limp, Stack heard a tearing sound behind him. He released the dead Comanche and moved to the back of the teepee as a knife finished cutting a long rent in it. When a head poked through, Stack had his leather thong ready, but he recognized Jack Pike, who had a rather surprised look on his face.

*   *   *

Pike was directly behind one of the teepees. He laid his rifle down and took out his knife. He used the point of the knife to make a hole, then forced the knife farther through the fabric of the teepee and began to cut through it downward. In the quiet night, the sound of the tearing fabric sounded obscenely loud.

Pike poked his hand through the tear he'd made, and the first thing he saw was a dead Comanche lying on the floor of the teepee. He turned his head to the right and saw the ghost of Joe Stack. The man was filthy, covered from head to toe with dirt, and clad only in a G-string. His skin also had bloody patches, as though he had been dragged.

"I came to rescue you," Pike said. "I see I didn't have to bother."

"All help is gratefully received," Stack said. "Come on in."

Pike entered the tent and checked the prone Comanche to make sure he was dead.

"There's one other tent with a brave in front of it," he told Stack.

"That is where they are keeping Walking Star."

"Is she all right?"

"They had her in here for a while, but they took her out earlier today to take her to Strong Elk. I have not seen her since."

"Well, if they have a man stationed in front of her teepee she must be alive. How are you doing? You look like shit."

"I've taken some lumps," Stack said. Pike could see the bruises and scabs that were spread all over Stack's torso and legs.

"Can you travel?"

Stack nodded. He was so filthy that the whites of

146

his eyes shone from his dirty face like the moon shining from a night sky.

"We have one problem," Pike said.

"What's that?"

"If anyone notices that this brave is gone they're gonna come over and investigate."

"So, we'll just have to move fast, before that happens."

"No, I have a better idea," Pike said.

"What's that?"

"We'll put him back."

"What do you mean, put him back?" Stack asked, looking puzzled.

"I mean," Pike said, bending over and taking hold of the Indian from beneath his arms, "we'll put him back out there, and nobody will be the wiser."

Stack saw what he meant then, and bent to help him.

CHAPTER THIRTY-TWO

Pike stuck his head outside to make sure no one was passing by, and then they pushed the dead Indian outside. They propped him up against the teepee so that he looked as if he were sitting with his chin down on his chest, dozing.

Back inside the teepee, Pike said, "All right, let's use the back door here and work our way around behind the other teepee."

Stack nodded.

As they slipped through the back door created by Pike, Pike could see how painful it was for Stack to move. He wondered if the man had a broken rib. He touched Stack on the shoulder.

Stack looked at him.

"I'll get Walking Star," Pike whispered. "Why don't you see about getting us some horses?"

Stack hesitated a moment, then said, "All right."

"We'll need five," Pike said. "Carson and McConnell are waiting by the water hole."

"Carson is alive?" Stack asked, obviously pleased. He had seen the arrow strike Kit Carson in the back, and had despaired for his friend's life.

Pike nodded and said, "We'll talk later. Let's move."

Stack nodded, and they split up.

Pike hadn't bothered telling Stack that he already had a horse, just in case they wouldn't be able to pick that one up.

Pike circled the camp until he was behind the teepee where he now felt sure they were keeping Walking Star. He duplicated what he had done behind Stack's teepee, slicing through it, and stuck his head through.

Walking Star had obviously heard the sound of the fabric tearing and, as he put his head through, he saw her staring at him. Her face changed from a look of puzzlement to one of pure joy.

"Pike—" she started, but he held his finger to his lips. She immediately fell silent and he beckoned her to come to him.

He had considered killing the brave who was seated in front of the teepee, but this way was better. The man would never know that they were gone.

He helped her through the tear in the teepee and then she hugged herself to him.

"Are you all right?" he asked.

She only nodded.

"Can you travel?"

Another nod.

"Good, come on," he said. "Stack is getting some horses for us."

He put an arm around her and led her away from the teepee.

Across from that teepee, in front of the one where Joe Stack had been held captive, the dead Indian brave had begun to list to one side. Slowly, gravity began to take over and he slid farther and farther over until he was lying on his side.

The brave in front of Walking Star's teepee, Bright Eagle, rubbed his face with both hands, trying to wake himself up, and then looked across the way to see if the other brave, Little Hawk, was having the same problem.

He saw the man lying down and naturally he thought he had fallen asleep.

If Strong Elk saw him sleeping, he would be in trouble, so Bright Eagle stood up and walked across to wake up Little Hawk.

He shook the man, and when he did not awake he turned him over so he could see his face. The man's tongue was protruding from his mouth and his eyes were wide.

He was dead.

Pike and Walking Star had just reached Joe Stack and the horses when someone in the camp began shouting, raising the alarm.

"Damn!" Pike said. "Come on."

Stack had five horses pulled out of the string. He mounted one while Pike boosted Walking Star up onto another one.

"Go!" Pike said. "Ride to the water hole. Kit and Skins are waiting there."

"But you—" Walking Star started to argue.

"Take her, Joe!" Pike told Joe Stack. "I'll be right behind you."

Stack leaned over and slapped the rump of Walking Star's pony hard. He then threw Pike a little salute and rode off after her.

Pike used his knife to cut the string that was holding the rest of the ponies, and then raised his

Kentucky Pistol and fired into the air, shouting at the horses at the same time. As the horses scattered, he held his by the mane, controlling it, and swung up on its back.

There were some braves already running toward him, so he took up his rifle and fired a shot into their midst, to discourage them. Since the Comanche did not know how many white men there were, they all scattered or hit the ground to avoid further shots.

The extra two horses Stack had chosen had also run off, but Pike never would have been able to lead them and ride hard. He started after Walking Star and Stack. At least they'd have three horses—if they reached the water hole alive.

Strong Elk came charging out of his teepee at the first sound of shouting, to find Bright Eagle was running toward him.

"What is it?" he asked the brave.

"They have escaped," Bright Eagle said, "and they have killed Little Hawk."

In anger, Strong Elk struck Bright Eagle, knocking him to the ground. At that moment another brave came running up to him.

"The horses, Strong Elk," the man said. "They have been run off."

"Fool!" Strong Elk said, speaking to Bright Eagle. "If they escape I will have your tongue."

Bright Eagle stood up, his eyes wide with fear.

"Get those horses!" Strong Elk shouted, and Bright Eagle and the other brave started running, calling others to help them.

Strong Elk had watched his braves play games with Joe Stack during that day. He had allowed himself to be lulled by Stack's apparent docile behavior. And the woman, Walking Star, had satisfied him so well that afternoon that he had allowed himself to think that he had sufficiently cowed her into obedience.

He would not be fooled by either of them again.

This time when he caught them, he would kill Joe Stack immediately, and make the woman watch.

He would then make her a gift of Joe Stack's heart.

PART FIVE

ON THE RUN

CHAPTER THIRTY-THREE

Pike rode all night, knowing that Stack and Walking Star were somewhere ahead of him—*hoping* that they were somewhere ahead of him.

He had not been able to circle around and pick up the horse he had ridden there, which was a shame. It was a good animal, and they could have used it to cross the Cimarron desert.

Well, they would just have to make do with three animals.

It was coming on dawn when Pike saw Stack and Walking Star waiting ahead of him. They had dismounted and were standing by their ponies.

"What's wrong?" he asked.

"Nothing," Stack said. "I—I just need to rest."

Pike could see the pain etched on Joe Stack's face, but didn't believe that was the reason they had stopped. Stack had probably given in to Walking Star's plea to wait a while and see if Pike could catch up.

"Well," Pike said, "have you rested enough?"

"I have."

"Then we've got some riding to do," Pike said. "I'm sure scattering their ponies didn't hold the

Comanche up all that much."

Stack mounted painfully, and Walking Star sprang astride her pony lithely. She was obviously very happy, now that Pike had caught up to them.

"Joe, you might as well lead the way," Pike said. "If I tried to we'd end up going in circles."

"I doubt that," Stack said, "but let's go."

Strong Elk's braves rounded up a half dozen of the scattered ponies within twenty minutes, and Strong Elk picked five braves to start out with him after Joe Stack and Walking Star and whoever had helped them escape. He had looked at both teepees, and had found the cuts in the back which, he correctly assumed, had to have been made from the outside.

"Find the rest of those horses and follow after us," Strong Elk ordered the rest of his braves.

To the braves who were riding with him he said, "If we do not catch them I will have all of your tongues."

The braves all nodded, knowing that their leader meant what he said.

At the water hole the waiting was starting to get to both Kit Carson and Skins McConnell. Also, they didn't relish sitting another day in the sun.

"How long should we give them?" McConnell asked.

"As long as it takes them to get here," Kit Carson said. "Besides, where do we have to go?"

They both knew that, even healthy, they'd have a hard time making it on foot. With both of them wounded the way they were, walking across the Cimarron desert was out of the question.

They both started the day with some water, drinking it and dousing their heads and torsos with it. They had finished the last of the dried beef jerky the day before and were trying not to think about how hungry they both were, or how worried about their friends.

They were trying to decide what to do with their day—"Should we sit over *there* or over *there*, today?"—when they both heard the sound of approaching horses.

"Sounds like company," McConnell said, picking up his rifle.

Kit Carson reached for his rifle as well, and they both took up positions behind a rock, waiting to see who would ride in to the water hole.

CHAPTER THIRTY-FOUR

On toward noon, Pike, Stack and Walking Star decided to ease up on the stolen ponies. The sun was high and hot and they still had a long way to go.

Pike was also worried about Stack, who seemed to be having trouble sitting erect. He was bent over the pony's neck, hanging on tightly to the horse's mane. He would have had an easier trip in a saddle, had they been able to reclaim the horse Pike had used to get there.

"Let's rest a minute," Pike said.

"No," Stack said. "I'm all right." His voice was tight with pain.

"Ease up, Stack," Pike said. "We've a ways to go and Walking Star needs a rest."

She started to protest, but Pike waved her off and she realized what he was doing.

They stopped and dismounted. Stack, holding his ribs, eased himself to the ground and grunted when his feet touched down. He immediately went to his knees, his arms wrapped around his middle.

"Broken rib?" Pike asked, crouching next to him.

"Yeah, I think so," Stack said. "I'm having some trouble getting my air."

"Try and relax," Pike said.

Pike knew there was nothing you could do with a broken rib except wait for it to mend. He just hoped that it was fractured and not totally broken. The last thing Stack needed was to have a piece of rib come poking through his side.

Pike went to Walking Star and said, "Are you all right?"

"Yes," she said, "I am now."

For the first time he noticed the bruises on her face, one on each side.

"He hit you?" he said, touching her face.

She took his hand and said, "It is nothing. I am glad you came for me."

"Did you think I wouldn't?"

She shrugged.

"Walking Star, I told you I would never leave you to Strong Elk. I am sorry he hurt you, and if I am given the opportunity I will kill him."

"No!" she said, gripping his hand tightly. "If you try to kill him, he may kill you. I do not want revenge. I only want to go away from here, with you."

"Do you want to go back to your people?"

"No," she said, shaking her head. "It has been a long time, and they would not take me back."

Pike didn't know what he was going to do with her once they got back to the mountains. As much as he cared for her, he was a man who lived alone. There was no place in his life for a woman—not permanently. He hoped she would be able to understand that, when the time came for them to part company.

Pike went to the three ponies now and checked

159

them thoroughly, to make sure they were sound. He wished he had something to use to fashion some makeshift reins for Stack. It might have made it easier for him to sit the horse for the duration of their trip.

"All right," Stack said, struggling to his feet, "let's get moving again."

"Are you sure you're up to it?"

"I'm not going to get any better sitting here," Stack said.

He tried to mount his pony and the pain was too much for him. Pike watched and waited.

"Pike?"

"Yeah?"

Stack looked over at him and said, "Help me get up on this beast, will you?"

'Sure."

Pike went over and gave Stack a leg up.

"Thanks," Stack said.

"Don't mention it."

Walking Star had already mounted, and Pike got up on his pony.

"You two go on ahead," he said.

"Where are you going?" Walking Star asked.

"I'm going to ride back a ways and see how big a lead we've got."

"You do that," Stack said, "and you'll cut into your own lead."

"I'll catch up."

"And you'll use up your pony doing it," Stack said. "I say we all stay together. We've got more of a chance that way. What do you say, Walking Star?"

"I agree," she said, lifting her chin and staring at Pike.

"You're outvoted, Pike."

Pike frowned, but decided not to fight it.

"All right, have it your way."

"Then let's move," Stack said, and started his pony.

He-Who-Takes-Many-Scalps came riding back to Strong Elk and the other braves, who were resting their ponies.

"We are not very far behind," he said to Strong Elk, "and they seem to be stopping a lot to rest."

"It must be for Stack," Strong Elk said, remembering the injuries his braves had inflicted on the man. "Well, we will not stop to rest anymore, and we will catch up to them."

"Should we not wait for the others to catch up to us?" the other brave asked.

"There are six of us," Strong Elk said. "More than enough to take care of an injured man and a squaw."

"There mut be someone else with them," He-Who-Takes-Many-Scalps said, "and he must be armed." He couldn't help remembering what had happened when, at sixty strong, they had tried to take seven armed men.

"They have no mules this time," Strong Elk said, "and they will not kill the ponies. No, we will take them this time, and I will kill Stack and whoever helped him escape."

"And the girl?"

"She is still mine."

"But—"

"I will not discuss it further," Strong Elk said. "I have made my decision."

He shouted for his braves to mount, and then led the way at a gallop.

He-Who-Takes-Many-Scalps took up the rear, not

convinced that his leader was completely rational. Going after the girl—and Joe Stack—had already cost the Comanche much pride and many lives, including those of Black Bear and Hawk Moon.

Would Strong Elk not rest until he had destroyed the whole Comanche nation?

CHAPTER THIRTY-FIVE

Just when it seemed as if they were moving along well, despite Stack's injury, Walking Star's pony suddenly stepped into a hole and went down. Walking Star went tumbling over the horse's head and landed hard.

Stack was riding in front of her and didn't see it, but Pike was behind her and watched it all. He saw her fly over the horse's head and land with a sickening thud on the hard ground. As he hurriedly dismounted, he hoped against hope that she had not landed on her head. When he bent over her and turned her over, he saw the blood on her scalp, and the trickle from her mouth, and knew that she had.

"Walking Star," he said, holding her gently.

Her eyes fluttered. She said, "Pike . . . do not leave me," and then closed them.

She was still breathing, which might have been more of a curse than a blessing. Pike had seen people with head injuries linger on for days before dying. Sometimes it was better that they died immediately.

Stack came hobbling over and said, "Her horse's leg is broken. We should shoot it, but I don't think we should risk the shot."

Pike knew that Stack didn't have his knife, so he took out his own and handed it to him.

"How is she?"

"She cracked her head pretty good," Pike said, looking up at Stack.

Stack stared down at the girl in Pike's arms, then shook his head slowly.

"She's got guts," he said, and went to take care of the horse.

Pike knew it would take more than guts for Walking Star to survive. He had his doubts as to whether or not she'd ever open her eyes again.

Pike and Stack sat huddled around Walking Star, trying to keep the sun off her face. Pike had told Stack to keep going, but Stack had refused.

"Give me your rifle," he'd said, "and I'll keep watch."

"Joe, we're just waiting for her to die," Pike said. "I can do that alone. Go on, I'll catch up."

"Give me your rifle."

Pike gave Stack the rifle and Stack turned around so that he was still shielding Walking Star from the sun, but was able to watch behind them.

"This is silly," Pike said. "If the Comanche come riding up on us, how many of them do you think you'll get with that?"

"How many shots does this thing fire?"

"Just one."

"Then I'll get at least that many."

Pike stared at Stack. That was probably the first joke he'd heard the man make since he'd met him.

*　　*　　*

Pike kept staring down at Walking Star's lovely face, willing her to open her eyes. If she opened her eyes, he told himself, she'd live. In the past, when he had seen people with injuries like this one, they never opened their eyes again. Some of them lingered on for very long before finally dying, but never had any of them opened their eyes again.

If she could only open her eyes . . .

"Come on, Walking Star," he whispered, bending over her, "open your eyes."

"What?" Stack said.

"Oh, nothing. I was just . . . talking . . ."

"Oh," Stack said, turning his head around.

A few moments of silence went by with Pike silently imploring Walking Star to open her eyes.

"Pike?"

"Yeah?"

"There's another option here."

"Which is?"

"We could both leave."

Pike looked at Stack and said, "She asked me not to leave her."

"She would never know, Pike," Stack said. "We have both seen this kind of injury before. There is little chance that she will ever open her eyes again."

"I know that," Pike said. "But if we left she might not know, but I would. Why don't you go on ahead? Kit and Skins will be waiting at the water hole."

"I'll wait," Stack said.

"For what?"

"For her to die, or for the Comanche to come," Stack said, and then added with a shrug of his shoulders, "whichever comes first."

"Why is it I never noticed your sense of humor before?" Pike asked.

Stack looked at Pike in surprise and said, "Because I don't have one."

"That's what I thought."

"What's taking them so long?" Stack wondered. In an hour it would be dark.

"Why should they rush?" Pike said, stroking Walking Star's hair. "We're not going anywhere."

"Right."

"How are your ribs?"

"Fine, as long as I'm not moving."

"At least we're accomplishing something, then."

"What?"

"You're not in pain anymore."

"I didn't say I wasn't in pain," Stack said. "I said I was fine as long as I didn't move."

"Then it does hurt?"

"Yes."

"But not as much as when you move?"

"Right."

"I've never had a broken rib myself," Pike said, "although I understand it can be very painful."

"Yes, it can," Joe Stack said. "You can take my word for that."

Pike looked down at Walking Star and for a moment he thought she had stopped breathing. He leaned over, watching her, and then saw a pulse in her throat and a slight movement of her nostrils.

"Maybe she won't die," Pike said.

Stack looked at her, and then at Pike. They had stopped the bleeding from her head, but she had shown no signs of regaining consciousness, and her skin was cold and waxy.

"Maybe," Stack said, without much conviction. He was sure that Pike didn't believe that, either.

166

"And if she does," Pike said, "how are we going to bury her in this hard ground?"

"We're not," Stack said. "If we had time—and the makings—we could build a pyre for her, but we won't even be able to do that."

"Then we'll take her with us?"

"Sling her over the side of a horse?" Stack said. "Where's the dignity in that?"

"Where's the dignitiy in dying?" Pike asked.

"There is none, so what does it matter what happens to our body after we die?"

"I don't know," Pike said. "I don't know."

"I don't know, either," Stack said. He turned his head to watch for Comanche.

"I guess we're just making conversation."

"I guess so."

"Waiting for this poor, lovely creature to die."

"Uh-huh."

Pike looked down at Walking Star and would have spoken to her, except that Stack spoke just then. It was odd how gentle his voice was, considering what he had to say.

"Here they come."

CHAPTER THIRTY-SIX

Pike eased Walking Star's head off his lap and onto a folded blanket. He rose to his knees and took out his Kentucky Pistol.

"They've stopped," Stack said.

"How many?"

"Six."

"Strong Elk?"

"He's there."

"What are they waiting for?"

"They're taking stock of the situation," Stack said. "They know they've got arrows and lances against our weapons, and they remember what happened back at the mule fort."

"They're trying to decide which two want to die first," Pike said.

"Exactly," Stack said, "but I don't think that will hold them for long. After all, we are out in the open and unprotected, and they don't figure us to slaughter our horses the way we did the mules."

"Then we just have to wait for them," Pike said.

"We haven't got much else we *can* do, Pike," Stack said. "The next move is theirs."

"And it just might be the last move."

"Why are they just sitting there?" He-Who-Takes-Many-Scalps asked.

"One of them is injured," Strong Elk said. "It looks like the girl."

"Maybe she is dead," He-Who-Takes-Many-Scalps said hopefully. If the girl was dead, maybe Strong Elk would return to his senses.

"Perhaps," Strong Elk said. "And perhaps it is a trap for us."

"A trap? What kind of a trap? There are only two of them."

"They might be trying to draw us to them."

"There is no one else around, Strong Elk," He-Who-Takes-Many-Scalps said. "We should just ride up to them and kill them."

"All right," Strong Elk said.

"All right?"

"Yes," Strong Elk said. "Take the men and ride up to them and kill them."

"And you?"

"I will watch from here, for a trap."

"There is no trap."

"We will see," Strong Elk said. "Go, kill them. It will be you who counts coup this day."

"It is my honor," He-Who-Takes-Many-Scalps said.

He spoke to the other braves, and they all took up their lances and rode for the white men.

It never occurred to the braves that their leader might be afraid to ride with them. In fact, it did not even occur to Strong Elk. Over the years he had become expert at explaining to himself why his decisions and moves were not those of a coward.

"Now they *are* coming," Stack said.

"Here we go."

They both rose, Pike standing directly in front of Walking Star.

"Where's Strong Elk?" Pike asked.

"He is not with them," Stack said. "He has sent them ahead and is watching from behind."

The Comanche let out a war whoop as they approached the white men. Stack took up the rifle and fired, and one brave flew from his saddle.

Pike waited for them to get closer. He dodged a thrown lance and then fired at one of the other braves, who had not yet let fly and was still armed, rather than waste the ball on a brave who was unarmed. The armed brave fell from his horse.

Stack stepped forward, reversed the rifle and took a brave from his horse by laying the rifle right through his middle.

The remaining two braves rode past, then turned to ride back. Neither Stack nor Pike had time to reload, so they just stood and waited, holding their rifles by the barrel. The two braves saw this and took the time to draw their bows and arrows.

"This is it," Pike said.

They waited while the braves put the arrows to their bows and then took aim.

"Ever dodge an arrow?" Pike asked Stack.

"I've never even tried."

"Well," Pike said, "there's a first time for everything."

"And a last . . ."

Suddenly, there were other war cries and the sound of shots. Both Indians were thrown from their horses and struck the ground, dead. Behind them rode Kit Carson and Skins McConnell, screaming and hollering like blood-crazed Comanche.

Pike turned and saw one of the fallen braves moving in behind Stack with a tomahawk. He drew his knife, pushed Stack out of the way and drove the knife into the brave's stomach. The tomahawk struck his shoulder a weak blow, struck bone, and bounced off. The pain was at once sharp and numbing.

Stack turned and shouted, "Strong Elk!"

The Comanche leader, seeing what had befallen his men, had turned and fled.

When Carson and McConnell reached them, they all checked the fallen Comanche and found them dead.

"Where did you fellas come from?" Pike asked.

"Thought you might need some help," McConnell said.

"These two horses rode right up to the water hole," Carson said, "and they're not ours. I don't know whose they are, but we decided to put them to good use."

"You were supposed to go on across the Cimarron," Pike reminded them.

"I don't remember agreeing to that," Skins McConnell said. He looked at Kit Carson and said, "Do you remember agreeing to that?"

Carson shook his head.

"I don't recall agreeing to that."

McConnell looked down at Walking Star then and said, "What happened to her?"

171

"She was thrown when her horse stepped into a hole," Pike said. "She hit her head."

"Damn," Kit Carson said.

"We were just sitting here," Pike said, "waiting . . . she asked me not to leave her."

McConnell bent over her, then stood up and looked at Pike.

"She's dead, Pike."

Pike looked down at her, and was glad that she had never regained consciousness, and that she hadn't lingered even longer.

"What do we do with her?" he asked.

The others all exchanged glances.

"Pike, we have to leave her," Stack said. "Strong Elk will be back with the rest of his braves."

Pike kept staring at Walking Star, then looked at Joe Stack and said, "No, he won't."

"He won't?" Stack asked.

"No," Pike said. "Not if I catch him first."

"Pike, you're hurt—" McConnell said as Pike mounted one of the Indian ponies.

"I'm still in the best shape to chase him," he said. "If I can get him before he gets to the rest of his braves, we'll have a chance."

"Here," Kit Carson said, handing Pike his Kentucky Pistol. "It's loaded."

"Thanks," Pike said, tucking the pistol into his belt. "Go on to the water hole. I'll meet you all there."

"Pike," McConnell said, "good luck."

"Thanks."

Stack put his hand on Pike's knee.

"Kill him quickly," he said. "Make sure he is dead."

"I will."

172

Pike waved to the others and then sent his horse off at a dead gallop.

He *had* to catch Strong Elk, for all their sakes—and for the sake of revenge, for Walking Star, and for Joe Stack.

And for himself.

CHAPTER THIRTY-SEVEN

When Strong Elk saw his braves go down, his first instinct was to get away. This was because he was a coward, as Joe Stack had told the others, although Strong Elk himself would never admit such a thing.

To Strong Elk's twisted way of thinking, retreat was a thing of honor. Saving himself—their leader—was the most important thing, even if it meant a few braves had to die for him.

He was convinced that it had, after all, been a trap and now five more of his braves were dead. These four white men had already killed more than twenty of his braves.

It was obscene that four white men could kill that many of Strong Elk's people.

He had to get the rest of his men and ride them down. He had to crush them once and for all—especially Joe Stack, his mortal enemy.

Joe Stack knew something about Strong Elk that no one else knew. Stack had tried to convince Strong Elk's people that their chief's son had raped and killed their medicine man's daughter, but he had been unable to do so.

He would try again, though. Strong Elk knew that.

Unless he killed Joe Stack this time, the man would try to destroy him.

Strong Elk didn't know it—because it wasn't in him to think of such a thing—but a true chief would have ridden with his men, trap or no trap. A true leader would have died with his braves.

In his mind, however, he had done the right thing, for he was alive to be able to avenge the deaths of the five braves, who had been led by He-Who-Takes-Many-Scalps. When he found the rest of his people they would be able to take their revenge for their comrades properly, and make all of the white men suffer before they died.

Although his subconscious would never allow him to admit it, Strong Elk knew that Joe Stack had seen him turn tail and run. For that, and for everything that had been between them in the past, there was a burning urgency inside Strong Elk that told him that Stack had to die.

One way or another Joe Stack would die, and die screaming.

PART SIX

THE HUNTER

CHAPTER THIRTY-EIGHT

Pike pushed the Indian pony as hard as he could. There was no thought in his mind of saving enough of the animal to get back to the water hole. All he wanted to do was catch Strong Elk and kill him. He urged the horse forward with this single thought in mind.

He stared straight ahead, willing his eyes to see Strong Elk—and suddenly he did. It was a small spot, way ahead of him, but he knew that it was Strong Elk, running away, the way a true coward would. He knew that in Strong Elk's mind he was simply riding to find the rest of his braves, but all true cowards were convinced that they were not cowards. He had known men like that before, who deluded themselves into thinking anything they did was right, and anything others did was wrong.

Pike would make sure that Strong Elk knew he was a coward before he killed him.

Strong Elk did not know what made him look behind him, but he did, and he saw the rider approaching. He hadn't been pushing his pony up to that point, but he did now.

The rider was not Joe Stack; he could tell that much. It was the much bigger of the four white men who was chasing him.

Like a true coward, it never occurred to him to turn and fight.

Pike knew Strong Elk had seen him, and was urging his own horse on now, but he also knew that he continued to gain on him steadily. He didn't know if he had a faster pony or not. Perhaps he was only gaining on Strong Elk because the Comanche's pony was forced to carry the extra burden of its rider's cowardice.

Before long, Strong Elk was there in front of him, big as life and twice as ugly. He was within range of the Kentucky Pistol, but Pike didn't want to kill him that way. He wanted to talk to him first, about what he had done to Joe Stack's wife, about what he had done to Walking Star. She had not told him so, but he knew that Strong Elk had not only struck her, but raped her as well. A man with Strong Elk's past would not be able to resist.

Strong Elk was going to pay for what he had done to both women.

Strong Elk turned and looked behind him. The white man was so close to him that he could see the look in his eyes—and it frightened him. He felt his heart pounding, and told himself it was because of the excitement.

Strong Elk turned forward again, vainly searching the horizon for the remainder of his braves. With them he would make this white man suffer.

Where were they?

The tail of Strong Elk's pony was tickling the nose of Pike's pony.

"I've got you, Strong Elk!" Pike shouted.

Strong Elk's long hair was streaming behind him, and as Pike's pony edged up on the Comanche's, Pike reached out and grabbed ahold of it, and then pulled. He veered his pony to one side to add to the pull, and suddenly Strong Elk went backward off his pony.

Pike yanked on his pony's mane to stop him, and hurriedly dismounted. Behind him, Strong Elk was staggering to his feet, blood covering his face from where it had been scraped raw by the ground.

"I will kill you for this, white man!" he shouted in anger.

"That's what we're here for, Strong Elk," Pike said. "You are going to pay for what you did to Joe Stack's wife, and for what you did to Walking Star. Only one of us will walk away from this spot."

Strong Elk looked around him, for help or for a place to run, but neither was there.

"Come on, Strong Elk," Pike said, leaving his Kentucky Pistol in his belt. "Show me what a mighty, fearless warrior you are—or are you truly a coward, as Joe Stack has told me?"

"I will show you who is a coward, white man," Strong Elk said, taking out his knife.

"Good," Pike said, taking out *his* knife. "Come ahead, then, and show me—but remember, I'm not a woman whom you can bully. I'm a man and I'll fight back."

Strong Elk licked his lips, but there was no other way to go. Pike knew he had pushed the man into a corner, and he was going to have to fight.

181

Strong Elk screamed and charged Pike, his knife slashing. Pike sidestepped his attack and put his foot out. Strong Elk tripped and went sprawling into the hardpacked dirt. His knife was jarred loose and flew from his hand, landing several feet away.

Strong Elk turned over into a seated position, looking up at Pike with wild eyes.

"Pick up your knife, Strong Elk," Pike said. "I want this to be very fair."

Strong Elk looked for his knife, located it and scrambled over to pick it up. He got to his feet then, and faced Pike.

They circled each other for a while, slashing and jabbing, for the most part missing. Once Strong Elk got lucky and nicked Pike on the forearm, but Pike ignored the wound.

On the other hand, when Pike did the same thing to Strong Elk, the wound seemed to worry the Comanche. He wiped at it, as if he could close it that way and keep it from bleeding, however slightly.

"You're nothing, Strong Elk," Pike said. "Without your braves to back you up, you are nothing."

"I am Strong Elk," the Comanche said, "leader of my people."

"If I ever saw an Indian who was a con man, you're it," Pike said. "You've got all of your people hoodwinked into thinking you're somebody."

"I will show you who I am," Strong Elk said. "I will cut out your tongue."

"You know something, Strong Elk?" Pike said. "I've changed my mind." Pike straightened up and made a great show of putting his knife away.

"You surrender?" Strong Elk asked, hopefully.

"No," Pike said, laughing, "I don't surrender, Strong Elk, not to you. I was going to take you apart myself, for Joe Stack and for Walking Star, but I've

182

decided that you aren't worth the sweat I'd work up doing it."

"What do you mean?" Strong Elk asked, frowning.

Pike took the Kentucky Pistol from his belt.

"Wha-what are you doing?"

Pike moved closer to Strong Elk and pointed the pistol at him.

"I'm saving myself from wasting my time on you."

"You cannot," Strong Elk said. "You must fight me, like a man."

"A man fights like a man when he's facing another man," Pike said. "I'm facing a mad dog, and a mad dog you just shoot, flat out."

"You cannot," Strong Elk said. He looked down at the knife in his hand, and then tossed it away. "The law of your people says you cannot kill a man who is not armed."

"The law of my people is for men," Pike said, "not dogs."

"You cannot—" Strong Elk said again, but Pike buried his fist in the Comanche's midsection. Strong Elk folded up and fell onto his knees, his mouth open as he gasped for air.

Pike stuck the barrel of the pistol into the Comanche's mouth and pulled the trigger, blowing out the back of his head.

When Pike rode past the point where he had left Carson, McConnell, Stack and the body of Walking Star, there was a large burnt patch on the ground.

"They found a way to make you a pyre, didn't they, Walking Star?" Pike asked. "They must have taken the time to ride out and look for the makings. Well, at least you won't have to lie here and rot."

He dismounted and walked to the charred spot and

spoke to her remains.

"He's dead, Walking Star," Pike said, "and in the end his eyes were wide with fear. He paid for what he did to you, to Joe Stack's wife, to everyone he ever bullied. He was a Comanche without honor. I've never met a Comanche before, but I've known Indians before. Your own people the Crow, the Blackfeet, the Delaware, but I'd never known an Indian without honor and courage until now. Well, he's dead, and he won't poison his people any longer with his cowardice."

Pike stood up and mounted his Indian pony again.
"Goodbye, Walking Star."

EPILOGUE

ONE

When Pike rode up to the water hole he found Kit Carson, Skins McConnell and Joe Stack waiting there for him. They were a ragtag threesome, filthy and bandaged and looking half dead.

He was never so glad to see anyone in his life.

"Glad you made it," McConnell said.

"Nice to see you," Carson said.

Pike dismounted, walked his horse to the water, and then helped himself to some.

"Is he dead?" Stack asked.

Pike stood up and turned to face Stack.

"He's dead."

"How?"

Pike told him how he'd put his pistol in Strong Elk's mouth and watched the fear grow in the man's eyes before he pulled the trigger.

"In the end," Pike said, "he knew what he was. I'm sure of it."

"He's dead," Stack said. "Good. I would have liked it if he had suffered, but it was good you killed him quick. It is what I should have done long ago. It is what he should have done with me."

Stack walked away and Carson and McConnell came over to Pike.

"I want to thank you fellas for seeing to Walking Star," he said. "Must have taken you some time to gather up the makings for that pyre."

"Took us a little while," McConnell said, "seeing as how we're all beat up and all."

"Yeah, well, thanks," Pike said. "How are we doing on horses?"

"Well, we've got five, which means we've got an extra," Kit Carson said. "That's a luxury I don't know if we can stand."

"We'll do the best we can," Pike said.

"You fellas think we can get across the Cimarron back to the civilized world?"

"You mean the mountains?" McConnell said.

"That's what I mean."

"Pike," Kit Carson said, "after what we been through, I think that'll be a cinch."

TWO

Skins McConnell was once again sharing a bed— or a floor—with Gina. She had been very glad to see him, and had practically dragged him into her tent. She clucked over his wound, which had healed rather nicely, and told him that she would make him feel better.

McConnell lost himself in the scent and the taste of her, the feel of her smooth skin beneath his lips as he kissed her small, taut breasts and nibbled her turgid nipples.

Her hands were urgent on him as she took hold of him and stroked the length of him until he could no longer resist. He pushed her down onto her back, mounted her and drove himself into her, and all the horrors of the plains faded away.

It was good to be back in the mountains.

Jack Pike and Kit Carson were at the saloon tent, a cold beer for each of them.

"I still don't understand," Pike said.

"What?"

"Why Joe Stack chose to remain on the plains instead of coming back here with us."

"With Strong Elk dead, Joe wanted to go back to his wife's people. Even though you killed Strong Elk, he still wanted to try and make the Comanche understand what a coward Strong Elk was."

"Well, if they'll listen to his story with an open mind and an open heart, I'm sure they'll come to that conclusion," Pike said.

"I hope so. What are your plans, now?"

"I'm going to go high up in the mountains with Skins and stay there for a while."

"Sounds like a good idea," Carson said. "Would you like some extra company?"

"Sure," Pike said, "but I don't think I can promise you as much excitement on this trip as you provided for me on yours."

"Please," Kit Carson said. "I've had enough excitement to last me . . . well, at least a year."

Pike walked over to the trading post when it was near closing time. As the last customer of the day walked out, he walked in.

"I'm sorry," Angelique said, her back to him as she put something back on a shelf, "but we are about to close. You will have to come back tomorrow."

"What I want," he said, "you don't sell here."

He saw her pause, and then she looked over her shoulder at him.

"Pike!" she said, turning around quickly. He had the impression she would have liked to throw herself into his arms, but she was holding herself back.

"How long are you here for?" she asked.

"Not long, Angelique," he said. "Just long

enough to say hello and goodbye."

She stared at him for a few moments, and then said, "Well, I suppose that is good enough. Some men don't even do that. Lock the door, will you?"

They were in her house, in her feather bed, and she was atop him, riding him. She leaned over so that her breasts dangled in his face, and he teased them with his tongue. He reached for them and brought them together so that he could suck both of her nipples at the same time. A woman's breasts had to be large enough for a man to be able to do that, and Angelique's were a prime example of that.

He was buried in her to the hilt, and the heat he felt inside of her was like the heat of the plains.

She had her hands pressed flat against his chest as she continued to ride him up and down, and when her time finally came she threw herself prone on him, her large breasts flattened against his hard chest. He reached for her plump buttocks and held her tightly to him as he exploded inside her . . .

"Tell me the truth," she said.

"All right."

"Why did you come back?"

He thought for a moment of Walking Star, and of what had happened on the plains.

"Truthfully?"

"Yes," she said, "truthfully."

"I wanted to forget the past few months," he said. "I wanted to come back and start my life over again, from here."

"Was it that terrible?" she said, touching his

wounded shoulder.

"Yes."

"No memories worth keeping?"

Again, he thought of Walking Star, of her loyalty, her tenderness, of her honesty.

"Well," he said, "maybe just one."

GREAT BOOKS

E-BOOKS

AUDIOBOOKS

& MORE

Visit us today

www.speakingvolumes.us

www.ingramcontent.com/pod-product-compliance
Lightning Source LLC
Chambersburg PA
CBHW050732250626
47155CB00005B/1766